Ghosts of the Shephelah, Book 6

Dinah

Ghosts of the Shephelah, Book 6

Dinah

JAMES K. STEWART

RESOURCE *Publications* · Eugene, Oregon

GHOSTS OF THE SHEPHELAH, BOOK 6
Dinah

Resource Publications
An Imprint of Wipf and Stock Publishers
199 W. 8th Ave., Suite 3
Eugene, OR 97401

www.wipfandstock.com

PAPERBACK ISBN: 978-1-6667-3846-9
HARDCOVER ISBN: 978-1-6667-9920-0
EBOOK ISBN: 978-1-6667-9921-7

MARCH 8, 2022 10:53 AM

This book is dedicated to my daughter, Shelly Lynn Ettrich,
a high-spirited, zealous prayer warrior.

Contents

Acknowledgments

THE STUDY OF SCRIPTURE has been a richly rewarding experience. As a rebellious youth with an abusive father, I left high school with a grade ten technical education. Without any knowledge of scripture, I had no idea of the blessings derived from a faith belief in God.

My journey to ordination began when I became a member of a fraternal organization. On completion of my initiation, I was presented with a Bible. The precentor asked if I was familiar with its contents. Before I could answer, he continued. That simple question changed my life. As a result of that one question, I have read the Bible, cover to cover, several times, in various translations. A few years later, I was asked to become a member of our church session. After ordination as a ruling elder, I was partially instrumental in convincing the church to sell its small community church building and build a large regional church on the main street. The years passed. Our new minister asked if I would like to preach a sermon for whatever reason had motivated him. I agreed. Needless to say, it led to seminary and ordination as a minister. Having obtained a Master's Degree, the quest for knowledge led to a doctorate.

In retrospect, the many blessings of family and friends are my most valued treasures. In light of those blessings, I would like to thank all those who have helped and supported me. Ghosts of the Shephelah result from what faith in God and the blessings of friendship can accomplish.

REV. DR. JAMES K. STEWART

Introduction

PLEASE ALLOW ME TO introduce myself. I am Dinah, one of the many Ghosts of the Shephelah. Daughter of Leah and niece to aunt Rachel, I was not the only daughter of Jacob, but apparently, the only one our oral tradition thought was worth mentioning. Please forgive my sarcasm, as, for sixteen years, my life was everything a young girl could hope. With a devoted mother and a loving aunt to guide and ten brothers to protect me, I felt truly blessed. Then it happened on my wedding night, the most amazing night of my short life. My brothers murdered my husband Shekem in our marital bed and dragged me away in total shock. Not only that, they murdered every male in Shalem. They claimed it was for raping me, but they were wrong. He did not rape me. Shekem loved me, and I loved him.

Now my ghost roams the shephelah with sisters and brothers of every age. We tell our stories to all who will listen. In addition, I've asked Delilah to retell the story of Samson in her words. You will find it most intriguing.

Chapter 1

Dinah: The Birth

ON THE NIGHT OF my birth, lightning flashed, thunder clapped, and rain came pouring from the heavens in torrents. Howling winds snapped the ties holding the red tent curtain closed. The flapping curtain spilled the washbowl over the birthing bricks my mother Leah was standing upon. Swaddling cloth, rags, and the squatting midwife, Shifra, were soaked. One of the attendants, Amah, dropped the ritual knife into the puddle of mother's broken water sack. The distractions caused Shifra to pick up the knife at precisely the exact moment of my arrival. *Thump*! I dropped into the soaking wet mess on the birthing carpet. Thankfully, mother was smart enough to squat lower at that exact moment.

As a young girl, it never failed to warm my heart when auntie Rachel would tell of that night. Not since my grandmother Rebekah's birth had there been such an upset in the heavens. Each time she would repeat the story, her voice would resonate with fear and excitement. It was as if it were burned indelibly into her memory. Rachel would speak of her older sister Leah; how she had given birth to many children, but how only six healthy boys and six fine girls survived before I came along. A tear would come to Rachel's eye as she told how Leah stepped down from the birthing bricks, squatted, and lifted me from the watery mess. How mother reached over and took Rachel's shawl and wrapped me, umbilical cord still attached, so that I would not chill. While everyone was floundering in a panic over the disaster, Leah calmly wiped my face clean. Finally, Shifra regained control of the situation, cleaned the ritual knife in freshwater, cut and tied the umbilical cord, slapped my bottom, washed and swaddled me, and then did something strange. She kissed me on the forehead. This telling was emotional for Rachel as she was two weeks away from giving birth to Yowceph, a son for Jacob.

Every few years, on my birthday, Rachel would tell the story in the red tent and, in the same way, to women new to the tribe. I never tired of putting my head on my mother's chest, my arms around her waist, and holding tight all through the telling. This warmth, this special warmth, shared between a mother and daughter, is something that must be experienced to be comprehended. Nonetheless, I had arrived, and like my grandmother Rebekah, had a destiny. What I could not possibly know was that my destiny was to roam the shephelah, a fate not accorded to Rebekah. It seems that each ghost on the Judean lowlands has suffered a tragedy, in one form or another. Thus, we must endure until men begin to see that women are created as equals, *zakar* and *neqebah*, in the image of our creator God. Now that you know a little of my beginning, allow me to continue with life on the lowlands and my dysfunctional family.

***

Leah, the eldest daughter of Laban, was the first wife of my father Jacob, grandson of the patriarch Abraham, the Hebrew (from beyond). No one knows why God chose Abraham, an ordinary man. After migrating from Mesopotamia, God called him to leave his father Terah and continue further south into the land Cain had possessed many seasons ago. Abraham was the twice great uncle of Laban. In this era, we believed strongly in intra-tribal marriages and multiple wives, especially for those blessed to carry on Abraham's line. Life was harsh, and infant mortality was high. This marriage practice may seem strange to some, but it is the Hebrew way.

Dinah: The Birth

Many years before my arrival, great gramma Rebekah sent Jacob to her brother Laban to find a wife. Mother remembers the day well. Jacob, awestruck with Rachel's beauty, walked right by her without a second glance. Rachel was standing behind Laban awaiting his arrival. It didn't take long for Jacob to find favor with Laban as he was well-skilled in animal husbandry. Much to the chagrin of Laban's sons, Beor, Alub, and Murash, Jacob was put in charge of the flocks. This responsibility prompted Jacob to ask for Rachel's hand in marriage. Laban considered that a refusal might result in Rachel running off with Jacob, and worse still, the loss of an excellent herdsman; so, he agreed; provided, Jacob work for him seven years, in place of a dowery.

Leah watched those two love birds swoon and run off to the hills behind Laban's back for seven painful years. The years passed, and the wedding was set for the spring full moon. The affair was elaborate. Surrounding tribes, mainly those who had benefited from Jacob's wisdom, heaped magnificent gifts upon him. The celebration went on into the night. Jacob, elated beyond his wildest dreams, consumed too much wine. That special moment having arrived, Rachel was sent to the wedding tent to prepare. Friends congratulated Jacob and wished upon him many fine sons. Speaking like a father, Laban walked, guided actually, Jacob to the marriage tent. After saying the fertility prayer, he blessed his son-in-law and tied the tent curtain.

Now I know what you are thinking. This union is a happy-ever-after love story. Not so. In the morning, the whole of the village was awakened by Jacob's screams as he stormed to Laban's tent. The shouting did not last long. Laban stood his ground against the verbal onslaught.

Pushing Jacob out of his tent, Laban began shouting, "Who do you think you are coming to my village and deciding you would by-pass tradition and marry my second born daughter. You wanted to marry one of my daughters; I gave you one for seven years' work. Leah is now your wife, and you cannot change that!" The chastisement quieted Jacob as he knew the custom was the same with his tribe. All he could do was mumble, "But I love Rachel; I want to marry Rachel." Laban, the old fox, saw more opportunity in Jacob's honest desire for Rachel, so he put his arm around his son-in-law and began walking him back to the marital tent. Along the way, he bargained, "If you love Rachel as you say, would you be willing to work another seven years in place of a dowery for her?"

"Wait another seven years?"

"The years will pass quickly, and besides, you have Leah; she is a fine woman and will keep you warm."

"I know Leah is fine, but her eyes always seem to be looking elsewhere when I speak with her."

"Eyes, smeyes; breasts, look at big breasts. Nurse many children. Rachel, not so much."

"Seven more years Laban, seven long years. No! No! No! Too long Laban."

"Fine woman Leah, fine woman. Young, strong, a fertile field waiting to be plowed."

Silence prevailed. Jacob turned. He saw Rachel looking from Laban's tent. Laban could see the longing radiating in his eyes, and I am certain Laban could see the same in Rachel's. What was ironic was that Jacob thought he was good at deceit, but he was no match for his uncle Laban, who began.

"Jacob my son; I can see that Rachel longs for you, and you for her."

"Yes, with all my heart."

"Then it's settled."

"What is settled? Laban, nothing is settled."

"Next full moon."

"What has the next full moon got to do with anything?"

"You give me word; seven more years of work; you marry Rachel on the next full moon."

"Are you serious Laban, I mean, really serious?"

"Yes, but a second condition."

"Condition, what condition? Do you intend to throw in a few sheep to sweeten the deal?"

"No, no, no." Laban insisted. "No sheep. You must continue to do your duty with Leah and father many children. She has wide hips, built for countless children."

"And what of Rachel?"

"Rachel will bear many children as well. The tribe must grow."

Jacob looked from Rachel to her sister Leah, who stood uninhibited in the tent opening. Clothed in a thin cotton shift, her breasts swayed back and forth seductively. When Jacob's eyes focused on her swaying attributes, she smiled; motioned with her head to come. Laban looked at Jacob and knew his night's experience with Leah had been pleasant.

To seal the deal, so to speak, Laban said, "Go. Go now, and I will give you Zilpah, Leah's handmaid, and Bilhah, Rachel's handmaid as concubines that you may always have a wife when the others are in the women's tent."

Jacob knew he must abide by the custom. He looked one last time to Rachel and then began walking to the marriage tent. Before he entered, Laban announced one final condition.

His voice turned sinister, "And you will work two more years for each servant. Four more years, Jacob."

Rachel watched Jacob enter the marriage tent and the curtain fall. She sat on her pillow and cried.

***

The next full moon shone on a less than an elaborate wedding affair. Rachel and Jacob were happy but not as excited as on the full moon of their first marriage. My mother, Leah, was happy even though she stayed in her tent during the wedding. After all Laban's traditional efforts to marry her off had failed, she was finally married through trickery. That didn't matter to mother. She had a husband. Plain but still attractive in a weary sort of way, Leah had what father called "lazy eyes." Laban now had one less concern in life. All his sons and both his daughters were married. His son-in-law was renowned for his animal husbandry. The size of his flocks and the quality of fleece were known throughout the region. Time, however, marched on, and Rachel remained barren.

Jacob was more than dutiful in his attempts to give Rachel a child, but try as he may, his efforts were fruitless. That was not the case with Leah and his concubines. Leah bore a fine healthy son within the first year and named him Reuben. Before twelve more full moons had passed, she bore another, and they named him Simeon. Between those births, Bilhah bore unto him a daughter named Nava. Zilpah's first child was stillborn but later bore a girl they called Levana. Jacob once said that every time he sneezed, Leah became pregnant, not so with Rachel. She remained barren.

Next came Levi and Judah, and I must say that Judah was the biggest, strongest, and most handsome of all Leah's children. During these years, Bilhah birthed another daughter named Chaya and two sons, Dan and Naphtali. After giving birth to four boys in a row, Leah birthed two fine daughters, Mazal and Tikva. They were as opposite as opposite could be. Mazal was short and large, while Tikva was tall and thin. She was even taller than Judah. The years rolled on, and Zilpah bore unto Jacob, Gad, and Asher, while Bilhah bore two more daughters, Aliza and Shira. Zilpah had one last child that lived. She was named Ora (light). After giving birth to Issachar and Zebulun, Leah said, "Now that I have borne unto my husband six sons, surely I will be exalted in his tent."

Laban was right; she was created to birth many children, and I might add, Leah never felt the pain of a stillborn child.

Feeling like the gods had blessed him beyond measure, Laban enjoyed eating the first meal of the day under the awning of his tent and watching grandchildren galore running and playing in the village. With his three sons married and their wives bearing many children, it wasn't easy to keep the children's names straight and the parents to whom they belonged. Remembering was not the case for Rachel. She was still barren. When the time for the next women's cycle came, something happened. After bearing so many children, Leah ended up on the same cycle as Rachel. They had to spend the same days in the red tent. On the last day, Leah took Rachel in her arms and prayed. Unbeknown to Rachel, Leah had learned of Elohiym from Jacob. After the next cycle time had elapsed, neither Leah nor Rachel had come to the tent. Mother was as excited as her sister Rachel, well, almost as excited.

This absence signaled the time of my arrival. Two weeks before Rachel bore her first child, lightning flashed, thunder clapped, the wind howled, and *Thump*, I dropped into this world. For some reason, Jacob named me Diynah, which in Hebrew means "judgment." Rachel was there to watch, but that was all she could do with her size. When Rachel's time came a week later, the whole of the village gathered around the central fire. Jacob was as nervous as any father could be. Laban was the same. Finally, his beautiful young daughter was about to give birth. Somehow, Leah's prayer had not only broken the barrenness; it had cleansed Rachel's heart of the repressed bitterness she felt toward her sister.

The sky was clear; stars filled the heavens, not a leaf rustled in the trees the night Rachel stood on the birthing bricks for the first time. Leah steadied her by the side. Shifra squatted on the birthing blanket, one hand on Rachel's knee, the other monitoring her dilations. Everyone had worried that the birthing would be long, painful, and problematic after the many years of barrenness. It was not. When that long-awaited moment arrived, Rachel closed her eyes, took a deep breath, and pushed. A moment later, Shifra lifted, for all to see, a perfectly formed and healthy baby boy. When Jacob heard his son's first cries, he knew all was well. Turning to Laban, he said, "The LORD has added another child to my family. Halleluyah!"

The atmosphere was exhilarating that night as Shifra cut the umbilical cord, washed and swaddled the newborn child while attendants washed and dressed Rachel. Propped up on a bed of pillows, Rachel could not hold back her tears of joy as Shifra placed the newborn in her arms. Leah whispered to her sister, "You have the most beautiful baby boy ever."

Overjoyed, Rachel proclaimed, "After all these fruitless years, the gods have finally blessed me with a beautiful, healthy son."

Mother whispered, "Elohiym Rachel. Elohiym has blessed you."

Speaking softly, Shifra said, "When you are ready, I will take the child to Jacob so that he may name him."

Moments later, Rachel spoke. "It is time."

Bayla, one of the attendants, stepped out of the tent and held open the curtain. The village went suddenly silent. Shifra stepped out, holding the infant close. Deciding to add to the drama, she waited before approaching Jacob. Removing the head covering, Jacob could see that he had a healthy child.

Shifra spoke in a loud voice, "You have a healthy baby boy Jacob, congratulations."

His reply surprised everyone. Tears flowing, he inquired softly, "Rachel, is Rachel in good health?"

Shifra said later that she could hear his heart pounding. Even though Leah was his first wife, Jacob always considered Rachel his prime wife.

Surrounded by her six sons, Leah spoke softly, "Reuben, I fear this child will receive your birthright and your blessing."

This foretelling did not sit well with Leah's sons.

Chills still run down my spine when I tell how Simeon said to Reuben, "Don't worry, we'll not let that happen."

From that moment on, Jacob evoked the jealousy of his sons with all the special attention and gifts lavished upon Rachel's child. Unbeknown to Jacob, Laban had been watching the reaction of Leah's sons. The boy's reactions invoked a tinge of fear in Laban as he remembered his youth and the special attention Rebekah had received from Bethuel. This special attention did not create a problem for him as Rebekah was a girl and never threatened Laban's inheritance.

Lost in the emotional grandeur of the moment, Jacob bowed his head in silent prayer. Lifting the child to the heavens, he began the naming.

"Creator God. LORD of all. You have added to my house and given me another son of my loins. I name this child Yowceph (Yehovah has added) and pray your blessing upon him."

By this time, Bayla had helped Rachel to the tent entrance.

She said to herself, "*Yowceph, a fine name for my beautiful son.*"

Chapter 2

The Deceit

WITH LIFE AS IT should be, Laban could not have been happier. His sons and his daughters married, more grandchildren than a man could desire, flocks, the envy of the region, and Rachel's child, her only child growing tall and strong. It pleased Laban how Yowceph never grew tired of learning. The young lad came to him if Rachel or Jacob could not satisfy his curiosity. A great source of pride for any grandparent. Never before had Laban met or known anyone with such a hunger for knowledge, save, of course, his sister Rebekah. Yowceph was not as vivacious or high-spirited as Rebekah but was every bit as intent on the acquisition of knowledge. As the child grew, Laban would not hesitate in asking, "What do you think of this, Yowceph?" Or, "What do you think of that?" He was always impressed with the boy's depth of perception.

In consideration for his skill as a herdsman, Jacob had made an agreement with Laban not long after his marriage to Leah and Rachel that a portion of the flock would be given to him as wages. These sheep would enable him to build a flock to support his family, which was to come. The problem was, each time Laban saw how well Jacob's flocks were doing, he changed the terms of the agreement. Finally, Jacob took Leah to sit as a witness with Laban.

Jacob began, "For the last eighteen years, you have changed our agreement ten times. Each time, taking the healthiest and strongest into the flocks managed by your sons."

"Jacob; Jacob," Laban tried to console, "don't look at it that way. Look at all I have given you."

Speaking brisque and to the point, "Look at all that I have given you!"

"I appreciate what you—"

"No more appreciation," snapped Leah.

This shocked Laban.

My mother was not Jacob's first choice, but he had always treated her with dignity and respect. I always knew my father loved my mother. What more could a child ask?

Jacob continued, "From this point forward, every lamb born pure white will be put with your flocks. Every lamb born speckled spotted or black will remain mine. In that way, there can be no mistakes and no more changes."

Not liking being put on the spot, but with his daughter present, especially with her using every ounce of strength to focus both eyes on him, Laban reluctantly agreed.

Much to his surprise, Leah spoke up once again, demanding, "Give him your sandal father. we will keep it as a token of your pledge."

This mistrust hurt Laban, but he had no choice; his repeated lies had finally caught up to him.

Shortly after that, Jacob called a family meeting in the meadow where his flocks were grazing. He told the older children that from this day on, they would collect green branches from poplar, almond, and chestnut and strip the bark from them. When the children inquired "Why," he explained that by putting those branches into the water during the breeding season, the sap affected the purity of the fleece."

Reuben asked, "How father?"

"When the water is clean and fresh, the lambs are born with pure white fleece. Over the years, I have noticed that when these particular branches are in the water during the breeding season, the lambs are born speckled, spotted, or black."

To show her support, Leah added, "These will be the lambs we keep for your inheritance."

"But spotted lambs' mother," Simeon questioned, "are not white lambs more profitable?"

Quick to answer, Jacob said, "Yes they are, and when we come to our new land, we will graze the flock near clear streams, and when they breed, the lambs will be white."

"Even from the speckled and spotted?" asked Reuben.

At the same time, Leah and Jacob answered, "Yes!"

Leah made sure that all the children knew this was to be kept secret. When breeding arrived, branches were gathered and tossed into the water. While the children talked amongst themselves, Yowceph asked, "What about Laban's sheep? Will they not drink of the tainted water as well?"

"Yes," snapped Rachel, much to everyone's surprise, "Laban has deceived Jacob once too often. Now we will be the ones to deceive him."

And so, it went. Throughout the next two breeding seasons, most of the lambs birthed were either speckled, spotted, or black. Jacob had to take dozens of white lambs to clear water to ensure that enough lambs would be pure white.

***

Unaware of the conspiracy brewing, Laban had become complacent in his oversight of the flocks. His sons, happy with the luxury the flocks brought to the family, were oblivious to the changes. Fortunately for Jacob, the flocks tended by Laban's sons were three days travel to the north. This particular season, Jacob decided to start shearing the flocks early. At the end of the week, buyers arrived to view the bundled fleece. By mid-day, the last of the bails of wool had been loaded onto carts. While the merchants from Damascus readied themselves to depart, Laban arrived to see Jacob holding two pouches of silver nuggets. After complementing

Laban on the quality of wool, the merchants began their journey home. Jacob handed Laban the smaller pouch.

"What is this?" Laban asked, visibly upset. "Your pouch is larger."

"Look at the flocks Laban; there are more speckled than white."

"This is not right!"

"What is not right, father?" Leah demanded.

Mother knew what Laban was thinking and saw that he was again trying to squirm his way out of their agreement.

"Do you want me to get your sandal?" she asked sarcastically.

"But the flock," Laban muttered, "the speckled and spotted far outnumber the white."

"Laban," Jacob said softly, trying to calm his father-in-law, "I have worked fourteen years for your daughters and six years to build a flock for my family."

"Yes, I know. But your flocks—"

"You have changed his wages ten times. I will not allow you to change his wages again," snapped a supportive Leah.

Laban never really understood how much my mother loved my father. By this time, Rachel, Zilpah, Bilhah, and the children had gathered around Jacob and Leah.

Outnumbered and feeling deceived, Laban said, "I shall leave for the north immediately and discuss this matter with my sons."

Laban turned and stormed away. Jacob looked into the eyes of his family. Nothing needed to be said.

Leah's sons returned to the flocks and separated the white from the spotted. The women and children began packing family belongings into the carts. Servants broke down tents and loaded them onto carts. While this was happening, the older children had started Jacob's flock moving south. Four elderly shepherds, incapable of undertaking a long journey, volunteered to stay and tend Laban's flocks. The family was well organized, and by late af- ternoon, all that remained in the valley were a flock of pure white sheep and four elderly shepherds. While the women were pack- ing personal items, Rachel had slipped unnoticed into her father's tent, collected the family idols, and loaded them onto her camel. The trek south was underway, and for the first time in many years, Jacob's mind began to consider his brother Esau.

By the time Laban returned and found his family had run off with what he still believed were his flocks, it had been nine days. On the morning of the tenth day, Laban and twelve armed servants mounted camels and took chase. To add insult to injury, Laban found that his household idols were missing. The trail was not hard to follow, but he could not believe how far Jacob had traveled. Catching the fleeing Jacob at mid-day, Laban's servant surrounded the family. Immediately Laban's accusations began.

"What is this you have done; stolen away with my daughters, as captives taken with the sword? Did you not think I would desire to kiss my daughters and children one last time?"

Jacob admitted to his fear by saying, "I was afraid you would not allow us to leave, especially with the flocks I had worked so hard to build."

"But Jacob, I have been good to you."

Jacob replied, knowing not to raise his voice, "And I have made you a rich man in return."

"Mine, all mine. Look at the size of the flocks you have stolen from me!"

Leah, not willing to be misled by Laban's conniving, shouted, "Your flocks," jumped to her feet and pointed, "look again father! Not one sheep belongs to you."

Turning to his servants, Laban said, "Go look. Inspect the flock. Count the number of pure white sheep." Laban dismounted his camel, put out his hand, and said, "My idols, return them at once."

"What are you talking about? The LORD is my God. I need no idols."

"Nonsense!" Laban replied, "My idols are missing. You stole them."

Jacob thought for some time, then said to our family, "My wives, my children, open your packs that the servants of Laban may search." Turning to Laban, he said, "Search, that you may know that I am not a thief."

Jacob's wives, sons, and daughters dismounted and aided Laban's servants in searching each pack. The supply cart was searched, and the carts with the tents, but the servant found nothing that belonged to Laban. Finally, everyone stood looking at Rachel. Still seated on her camel, one leg crossed over the other, she was not about to dismount.

Laban approached. "Please, my daughter, I desire to search your camel pack."

"O father," she began, "I am in the way of a woman. If I dismount, I will have to find a stream and clean myself immediately. I beg you, allow me to stay seated while you search through my belongings."

Laban respected her request and searched as best he could but did not find anything belonging to him. He was perplexed as he could not understand why his servants had not found even one idol. Jacob, relieved that nothing was found, still did not want to provoke his father-in-law further, so he invited Laban to sup with him and his family one last time. When Laban agreed, Rachel called to her servant to lead her to the nearby stream to wash. Taking cleaning clothes and a blanket from the cart, the servant girl helped Rachel to the creek and hung the blanket over a branch. Rachel, speaking with the servant as if being cleaned, used the cover-up to remove Laban's idols from her pouch and hide them in the dirty rag pack. While the servant returned the cleaning rags to the cart, Rachel led her camel to her father.

She said, "Here father, you may satisfy yourself that your idols are not on my camel or in my pack." Laban searched himself but found nothing that belonged to him.

My older brothers took bows and arrows to hunt along the stream. Quails, too lazy to fly, were easy prey. Rabbits, accustomed to the tranquil setting, were easy quarry. Servants netted unsuspecting fish. All the while, Zilpah and Bilhah took charge of building the fires, cleaning the wild game, and preparing the food. Jacob opened a skin of wine and invited Laban to sit.

Still disgruntled, Laban mumbled, "All that you have is mine."
"No," came the quick response from Leah, not willing to allow Laban any leverage.

It did not bother my mother that Jacob had three other women. It was the tribal way. One woman with many husbands could only bear one child a year. One man with several wives could produce many children a year and thus build tribal numbers. Besides, Leah could now hold her head high; she had many fine sons and a husband who never neglected the marriage bed. The hard-cold reality of our culture was that when a young girl passed a certain age and did not have a husband, the father gave up hope of a dowry. When that happened, the young woman was sold as a servant or a concubine. That is what had happened to Zilpah and Bilhah.

Laban's response to Leah was like that of a patriarch. Unwilling to relent, he said, "These daughters are my daughters, these children are my children, and all that thou see is mine: and what can I do this day to protect these my daughters, or these my children which they have born," taking a deep breath and looking around he uttered a sad, "nothing, I can do nothing." Jacob was wise enough to remain silent. Laban continued, "Now, therefore, come let us make a covenant, and let it be a witness between me and thee."

Laban had finally resigned himself that his family was moving away. Relieved beyond measure, Jacob could see Laban was genuinely saddened at losing his family.

Jacob took a stone, set it up for a pillar, and then instructed his sons to gather one stone per person to make a heap. Laban ordered his servants to find a thick straight branch, cut it a cubit long and carve it in the shape of a penis. The men followed instructions and set it up on the north side of Jacob's heap. Laban called the witness heap *Jegarsahadutha*: but Jacob called it *Gal`ed*. Therefore, Jacob named the place Gal`ed. Touching the pillar Laban had raised to the fertility god Tammuz, he proclaimed, "This place shall be called *Mizpah* (watchtower), and may the gods watch between me and thee when we are absent one from another."

Jacob laid his hand on his *gal`ed* and repeated, "May the LORD my God watch between me and thee when we are absent one from another."

Laban went on to say, "I swear by the gods of my father Nahor that I will not pass over your *Ga1`ed* to do you harm."

Jacob replied, "I swear by the LORD God of father Abraham that I will not pass over your pillar to do you harm."

In the hope that Laban would relent and allow Jacob to return to his brother, he had ordered an ewe lamb slaughtered earlier that day. Building a fire beside the *gal`ed*, he sacrificed the entrails at his altar.

Laban, breathing the heavenly aroma of the roasting lamb, said, "Surely, this aroma is pleasing to all of the gods."

Jacob thought to himself, "Little does he know, there is only one God."

Eating and drinking went on into the night. In the morning, Laban rose early, kissed his sons and his daughters, and blessed them. Still distressed over the loss of his idols, Laban departed and returned to Padan Aram, never to see his children again.

Chapter 3

Facing Esau

AFTER A TWENTY-YEAR ABSENCE from his village, from his tribe, from his land, Jacob was about to face the unknown; his brother Esau. Each day as he traveled to the River Jabbok, the fear of vengeance mounted. Jacob never considered Esau would have naturally inherited tribal leadership when he did not return with a wife.

Jacob prayed, "Deliver me I pray thee, from the hand of my brother Esau for I fear he will come to smite me."

When he had finished his prayer, Jacob called two of his servants. He told them to separate from the flock twenty lambs and ten goats. As a precautionary move, they would leave for Esau's village first thing in the morning. He hoped his brother would receive the animals as a peace offering. Jacob sent his two wives, his two concubines, over the ford in the Jabbok but remained alone on the opposite side out of fear.

Jacob's life had never been uneventful, but tonight was to be unforgettable. Overwhelmed with fear, he had not realized he'd fallen into a deep sleep. Waking in the middle of the night, the light of the moon shone as if it were day. A man, a stranger, in bright raiment, sat silently waiting for Jacob to orient himself. Relieved it was not his brother Esau, Jacob asked, "Who are you, stranger?"

"For now, all you need to know is *Malak* (angel).

"Why have you come?"

"To be sure."

Becoming annoyed, "Sure of what, and quit speaking in riddles?" Jacob said.

"To be certain you are brave enough for the task at hand and not that frightened little boy who failed to return home to claim his inheritance?"

Jacob had no idea with whom he was speaking.

"I am returning home," Jacob said with a touch of spite in his voice.

"You shall not speak to me in that manner of voice; you frightened little boy."

Provoked enough, Jacob lept across and began to wrestle with the stranger. Thus, it began. Back and forth, the advantage changed countless times. Each time Jacob would gain the edge, the stranger would flip him off. He became so intent on triumph; Jacob did not realize the stranger was allowing him to get the advantage to test his endurance. Nearing dawn, Jacob caught the stranger in a bear hug from behind.

The stranger said, "Dawn is breaking. Let me go."

"No!" demanded Jacob, "Tell me why you have come."

The stranger reached down and grabbed the hollow of Jacob's thigh, pulling it out of joint. Jacob shivered in pain. His grip weakened. He dropped to the ground but managed to maintain his grip around the stranger's ankles.

Satisfied with Jacob's fortitude, the stranger said, "Let me go, for the day breaketh."

Jacob knew he must undoubtedly be wrestling with a heavenly angel and cried, "I will not let thee go, except thou bless me."

The angel began, "What is thy name?"

"Jacob," came the reply.

Jacob felt the angel's hand light upon his head.

"Thy name shall be called no more Jacob, but Yisra'el (yis-raw-ale'). for as a prince hast thou striven with God and with men, and have prevailed."

Jacob asked, "Tell me, I pray thee, thy name."

"No!" came the reply, "but I will bless you."

Jacob released his hold on the angel and fell to the ground. Moments later, he opened his eyes. The sun had risen. All was calm. He looked around to see that he was all alone. Jacob called the name of the place *Penuel*.

Humbled, he said, "I have seen God face to face, and my life is preserved."

Jacob passed over the Jabbok to join his family. They noticed he now walked with a limp but would not explain how his thigh had been put out of joint. To this day, the children of Israel will not eat the hollow part of the thigh.

***

Jacob found it hard to believe that Esau could forgive and forget, so he devised a backup plan. He divided his family and possession in two and sent them off in different directions. He felt that if Esau were to capture one of the groups, he would meet the other at a predetermined location and continue to a new land. Little did Jacob know that Esau had come across the flock sent to appease his anger but rejected the gift. As Esau approached, Jacob moved to the front of his family and prepared to meet his brother. He got the surprise of his life. Esau, seeing Jacob, ran and put his arms around his brother, kissed him, and they wept. I could see father's fear evaporate at the gracious welcome. It was sad that Jacob had lived in fear all those years, but now that was in the past.

Looking over the people and flocks, Esau asked, "Jacob, who are all these people?"

Jacob replied, "This is my family and the flocks with which the LORD has blessed me. Come children," he shouted, "come meet my brother Esau."

I came forward with my brothers, mother Leah, and aunt Rachel. We bowed respectfully. When Esau met Yowceph, he immediately liked the young lad.

Esau asked, "What is the meaning of the flock you sent to me as a gift?"

"I wished to find grace in your sight, my lord."

Esau said, "I have more than enough, my brother; keep your flocks."

"Nay, I pray thee," replied Jacob, "if I have found grace in thy sight, and you are truly pleased to see me, accept my humble gift as my God has dealt graciously with me."

Jacob continued to urge Esau until he finally relented and accepted the gifts. It was as if everything I'd heard about Esau was wrong. Then it became clear.

"Father said to his brother, "You've changed."

Looking Jacob over, "So have you, my brother."

"I would never have guessed," Jacob replied, and a moment later, "but how?"

Esau told his brother of Rebekah's passing. That afternoon, she called him to her tent and confessed why she had favored my father. Tearful, she told Esau why God had required the deceit, but Jacob did not return with a wife. He had stayed in Padan Aram, and how the inheritance must of necessity fall to her eldest son. Esau admitted he began to cry.

Rebekah took her son's hand and said, "Esau, you are now the tribal chief. You must put your immoral ways aside and act like one. Remember, you are a child of God, and if you put your ways behind you, God will bless all that you do."

Esau told his brother how he put his head on Rebekah's chest and continued crying.

When he lifted his head, he said, "Mother, I will change; I promise."

Rebekah took his hand and kissed it.

Esau asked her, "What about Jacob?"

"I do not know my son, but I'm certain God will make another plan."

Esau told of how Rebekah's words had changed his heart and how he watched his mother take her last breath. It was an emotional reunion followed by a joyous celebration. The brothers took much pleasure in introducing their children to their cousins. Esau was proud of his eight sons, but the only one of Abraham's line was Reuel, the son of Mahalath, Ishmaels' sister.

Food was prepared and served. The brothers spent a heart-warming afternoon catching up and remembering. Late in the afternoon, Esau invited Jacob to return with him that they might resume living as brothers. Still, Jacob realized that disputes might break out with both having so much. Esau was saddened to lose his brother again but knew there was truth in Jacob's statement. So, Esau returned that day to Seir. Jacob journeyed to Succoth, to the city of Shalem. I should say at this time that mother and I watched Reuel carry on with Jacob's other daughters. Disgusted, and knowing what mother was thinking, I shook my head "no." Mother smiled and nodded her head in agreement.

After crossing the Jordan, mother and auntie went out to gather brown mushrooms around a lowland swamp. Auntie noticed mother had wandered too close to the bog and called out, "Leah, come back. The water is not good," but it was too late; mother had disturbed a nest of mosquitos. She ran, all the while swatting those pesky little insects, then tripped into the muddy bog. I sometimes think Noah should have swatted them when he had the chance. At any rate, it was not much longer before mother was suffering from *the fever*. Rachel was faithful in attending to her older sister. That night, Leah was burning up, and no matter how many times Rachel dampened the cloth, she could not knock the fever down. Somehow, mother found the strength to call myself and Rachel to her side. We knelt and took her hand.

Mustering every bit of energy, mother looked at me and said, "Do not let Jacob choose your husband." Looking to Rachel, mother said, "I love you."

Rachel was more taken than I because there had not been a time in my life when I did not know that my mother loved me unconditionally. Rachel choked up. Her head fell on Leah's chest, and she wept. Moments later, Rachel raised her head, sat up, put her fingers on Leah's throat, and said, "My sister sleeps with her ancestors."

The reality was, even though Jacob considered Rachel to be his prime wife, Leah was the first to marry. Leah's body was spiced and wrapped. First thing in the morning, her body was strapped upon a mule. We left immediately for Hebron and the Cave of Machpelah.

While placing mother's body on the stone slab, it was eerie to see the bones of Sarah piled beside those of Abraham; the bones of Rebekah piled beside those of Isaac. In time, Leah's bones would be placed beside those of her ancestors to await the wrapped body of Jacob to rest on the stone slab. I must say, Jacob was genuinely saddened at my mother's sudden death. His prayers finished; he was the last to leave the cave. As I watched servants pile the last rocks over the cave mouth, I realized that death comes to us all. I thought, "It doesn't matter how you die; what matters is how you live." My mother made the best of what she had, who she was, and as dangerous as it was for a woman to speak out against a man, Leah did just that to support her husband against her father. Jacob, Rueben, and Judah left for Shalem, as they had been negotiating the price of a piece of land with the local tribal chief. Hamor had freely offered Jacob the land to graze his flocks, but Jacob knew the value of owning land. Jacob remembered how king Abimelech continually ran his grandfather from one piece of land to the next until the tribe got to Beersheba. Abraham believed he had found the perfect place to feed his flocks and call home and hoped he would not get run-off in the future. It was peaceful beside the Bedor River but still too close to Gerar for comfort. Two full moons later, Abraham, still not comfortable, moved north to the slopes of the shephelah, near Hebron.

Mother had always been strong, and some of that had rubbed off on me. On the way back to Succoth, Rachel and I spoke of how the journey from Padan Aram had been long and arduous. Jacob's sons bartered fleece for olive oil and wheat, the necessities of life, whenever we made camp to rest the flock. Jacob always looked for the wine merchant; he loved his wine. Twice on the journey from Padan Aram, I was almost pledged to be married. Thanks to mother's inner strength, she was able to convince Jacob I'd not be happy with men who were no more than uncouth pigs. Sorry for the condemnation, but that was polite compared to how I could describe them.

By the time we arrived in Succoth from the burial, Jacob had purchased his desired parcel of land. He paid Hamor a hundred pieces of silver, piled round river rocks as an altar, and dedicated the land to *Elelohe-Israel* (the mighty God of Israel). Much to our delight, Jacob's sons were busy directing servants to set up our tent village. The two most essential items in any village are the central fire pit, complete with Y supports to hold the roasting spit, and the domed clay brick bread oven. It took eight men to drag a large flat stone, on which to knead bread dough, to a place near the bread oven. Jacob set his tent so that he could view the common area of the village. Now that he was aging, he loved to watch people work. Rachel became a second mother and confidant, and Yowceph, a great friend. We were the youngest, and I must admit, it was easy to get jealous over how Jacob spoiled young Yowceph, but that was how it was; I was a girl, he was a boy. Sadly, my older brothers did not see it that way.

For as long as I can remember, my brothers treated Yowceph as an adopted son. To them, he was a threat to Reuben's inheritance. The more Jacob heaped gifts upon Yowceph, his step-brothers heaped disdain. In the whole tribe, I was his only friend. Whenever Leah's sons bullied Yowceph, they received the wrath of Rachel as well as mine. And let me tell you, she could swing a mean walking staff. Many were the times when those boys limped home with bruised thighs.

One full moon after my mother's passing, I celebrated my sixteenth birthday. It was bitter-sweet. As I developed through my fifteenth year, I began to feel more like a woman than a girl. Men in the tribe noticed me more, always giving me a second look. Even my brothers stopped treating me like their little sister. Not to boast, but I had developed into a voluptuous, full-bodied, healthy young woman. To be honest, I began looking at men, young men, differently. When older men spoke, I knew what they were really saying, and sometimes it was disgusting.

Chapter 4

Meeting Shekem

YOWCEPH WOULD OFTEN RUN off by himself into the village of Shalem. He liked to meet new people and view the items for sale in the market. He was also getting to the age where he enjoyed chasing after the Hivite girls who flaunted themselves before this handsome young man. I had never made an issue out of it but had caught him admiring my attributes whenever he thought I was not looking. As I had said, my brothers would have nothing to do with Yowceph, so he found friends in Shalem. One of those friends was the son of the tribal chief, Hamor. His name was Shekem. One afternoon, while shopping in the market, Yowceph brought Shekem over to meet Rachel and me. He was handsome and strong, but I did not think much of a boy who could not speak. When I said, "Shalom," he just stood there with his mouth open. I could see Rachel holding back her laugh.

Yowceph understood why his friend stood silent, so he elbowed Shekem and said, "Say, Shalom."

Shekem took a breath, smiled, and said, "Shalom . . . you are beautiful."

I looked into his eyes and understood why he was speechless. I blushed.

Yowceph grabbed his arm and said, "Let's go to the river for a swim." Shekem didn't move. Yowceph pulled and said, "Come on. You've seen her; now let's go swimming."

The boys ran off.

That evening I went to Rachel's tent to talk about my feelings. Never having felt that depth of emotion, I needed someone with whom I could speak freely. She knew exactly why I had come.

Rachel began, "Leah told you about Jacob walking past her and straight to me when he came into our village."

"Yes, she did," I replied.

"Well then, let me tell you about the first time I met Jacob."

"That was not it?" I asked.

"Oh no. I was out in the pasture tending my goats. Late in the afternoon, I drove them to the well. My brothers talked among themselves and would not let me draw water as it was not the time. My brothers did love to tease me. I demanded them to move! One of the men, who I thought was one of our shepherds, stepped to the well and raised the water bag. He turned to face me."

"Did he say anything?" I asked.

"No, he didn't. I stepped very close, looked him in the eye, and said, 'I do not know you.'"

"Did he stand silent like Shekem?"

"No, he spoke, 'I am your father's kinsman. Son of Rebekah, your father's sister and you; you are beautiful.'"

I put my hand over my mouth and asked, "O my Rachel. What did you do?"

Rachel laughed and said, "Speechless for once in my life, I gasped. No one had ever surprised me like that."

"What happened? What did you do?"

"It wasn't what I did. Jacob cupped my face in his hands and said, 'You have my mother's eyes.'"

"What did you say?"

"I was breathless. I didn't say anything. I just dropped my staff and ran," Rachel answered.

"O Rachel, I hope Shekem comes for me."

Auntie and I talked late into the night. She understood my feelings completely but warned me that Shekem was not of our tribe and not of Abraham's line, so marriage was out of the question.

I was thankful for Yowceph and Rachel as they were the only two people I could trust to keep my feelings secret. During the following weeks, Shekem would have Yowceph arrange a place to meet, always chaperoned, of course. I hadn't ever imagined that love could be instant. I thought it was something that grew, that evolved after people got to know each other. I was wrong. I saw the love in Shekem eyes and, in an instant, my heart melted. We met often but grew tired of being chaperoned. I knew Yowceph felt it was a waste of time spending his day watching over us, and it was becoming laborsome for Rachel as she was with child. So it was, we set a time and a place. I left the village to go to the stream and wash but met Shekem once over the ridge.

When he saw that I had hoops on my ears and bracelets on my arms, he took my hand, and we ran to the stream where Shekem had spread a blanket. It was amazing to be alone with the man I had fallen in love with. While chaperoned, we'd only been able to sneak a kiss, but now, he looked deep into my eyes, took me in his arms, and kissed me as I'd never before experienced. It was incredible. We lay on the blanket. His weight felt awesome, and he delighted when I lay on top of him, but it did surprise him when I put my tongue in his mouth. Rachel told me that one, and wow, it was unbelievable. I could have lain in his arms forever, but fearing that my absence might arouse suspicion, we decided to part.

We stood. Shekem took my hand and said, "If I may, I will send my father to Jacob with an offer of a dow—

"Yes!" I replied before he could finish.

His eyes shone. We kissed, and I rushed back to my village.

Unbeknown to me, prying eyes had spotted Shekem and me running off, hand in hand. To make matters worse, they not only reported it to my father but to Simeon and Levi as well. Sadly, everyone believed the worst had happened. What was even more heartbreaking was how upset they were at the thought of having lost all chance of a substantial dowry. The following day, Hamor met with Jacob. He noted how Jacob's tribe had been a welcome addition to the landscape and how trading had benefited both. Jacob, not about to indicate he knew why Hamor had requested this meeting, agreed with everything said. Finally, Hamor got to the point by saying how much his son loved me. He relayed many of the statements Shekem had used to illustrate the depth of his love. Hamor rolled out a lambskin listing the extent of the dowry. Jacob was speechless but wondered why someone would pay any dowry for a defiled woman. It did not make sense. Jacob went on to explain to Hamor how Hebrew tradition dictates that those in the patriarchal line marry their nearest bloodline relative but that he did not see the need for that in Dinah's situation as the line, should by rights, pass through Rueben.

Hamor took Jacob's statement as a yes, and said, "Good, the matter is settled." He continued with, "There is plenty of time until the next full moon to inform relatives and invite guests."

Hamor parted with the good news for his son. Shekem was overjoyed.

The Marriage

Simeon and Levi hurried back to the village as fast as they could on hearing of Dinah's affair and the forthcoming wedding. They argued strenuously with Jacob, appalled that he would consider inter-tribal marriage to an inline descendent of Abraham. Simeon argued that Dinah must marry intra-tribal. Jacob knew that Dinah had not looked favorably upon Esau's sons. Levi noted that Esau did have a son of Abraham's line. Reuel was the son of Mahalath, the daughter of Ishmael.

Simeon said indignantly, "Ishmael is not of Abraham's line. Hagar was an Egyptian slave, a concubine."

"That is true, Simeon," Jacob countered, "but father Abraham did circumcise him. So, if a man is circumcised, does he not become one of Abraham's children?"

Simeon sat back, raised his hand to indicate he was thinking.

Lowering his hand, Simeon began, "If this prince is serious, then he and the men of Shalem must agree to our terms. They know that all Hebrew men are circumcised."

"So, what has that got to with Dinah's marriage," Levi asked.

"Everything," replied Simeon. "If Shekem wishes to marry into the Hebrew way, then he and every male in Shalem must be circumcised to become children of the covenant."

That would satisfy tradition," replied Jacob.

"Yes," noted Levi, "and we would get a substantial dowry for a sister who has played the harlot."

The word "harlot" caused Jacob to think for a moment and say, "The shepherd did not say he saw them do anything. All he saw was that they ran off holding hands."

Simeon snapped, "Why else would a young woman run off without her chaperone, holding hands and laughing."

Jacob went to reply but realized there would be no chance of changing Simeon's mind. It still makes me feel good knowing that my father had the faith that I would not defile myself and bring shame to our family. Shame, however, was the least of my worries.

Much to Levi's surprise, Simeon continued, "Father, I can see your mind is set. Go ahead and ask Hamor if the men of Shalem are willing to be circumcised. If so, we will proceed with the wedding."

Simeon and Levi left Jacob to his wine and returned to their flocks.

Once clear of the village, Levi said, "What is going on in that mind of your brother?"

"Our family has roamed enough Levi. It is time we settled in a village of our own. No more tents in the wilderness."

"But how?"

"I could tell by his silence that father does not believe Dinah would allow herself to be defiled."

"Neither do I," was Levi's response.

"Does not matter," Simeon said, "we can use this circumcision to our advantage."

"How?" asked Levi.

First, we spread the rumor that Shekem defiled the Hebrew girl Dinah."

"What good will that do? He wants to marry her."

"We will say the marriage is a pretense to cover-up the rape—

"But he did not rape Dinah; he only took her hand."

"The tribes will not know that."

"I still do not get the reason for the circumcision."

"We require Shekem to get circumcised long before the wedding as an act of faith, and so he will be able to perform in the marriage bed."

"And the surrounding villages?" inquired Levi.

We make sure the midwife does not get to Shalem until two days before the wedding. In order for the marriage to take place, the men will have to be circumcised.

"I still do not get it Simeon, why?"

Simeon stopped, looked around, and then said, "With the discomfort and too much wine, it will be easy for us to take them in the night."

"Take them," still confused.

"Yes. We kill all twenty-eight men of Shalem in their beds.

Levi finally smiled and nodded in agreement as he understood what Simeon was plotting.

I am sad to say that the plan was set. Fourteen days before the wedding, Shekem entered the red tent to be circumcised. Skeptical, the men of Shalem waited to see if there were any ill effects. There were none. Jacob sent for the midwife to return, but Simeon had made sure it was one of his shepherds that was the messenger. Finally, with only two days before the wedding, the midwife entered the village. She had taken a purse of silver in exchange for a story that would explain her delay. Her *izmel* (knife) and *barzel* (cutting guide) were kept busy all through the afternoon and into the evening.

The wedding was everything I had hoped. Like gramma Rebekah, I wore a long white gown with a white jasmine flower in my hair. Those with whom Jacob bartered had been invited to attend, as were other tribal chieftains and the friends and relatives of

Hamor. All I can remember of the ceremony is the words Shekem and I spoke, at the same time, "I do pledge." The banquet was unique as Hivite customs, traditions, and food differed from Hebrew. Nonetheless, it was all so very impressive. Jacob had supplied the roast lamb, and Shekem provided something I had only ever had once before in my life. It was beef, roasted the whole day over hardwood embers. It was so very delicious. Simeon, and much to my surprise, provided an ample supply of wine.

The men of Shalem, still tender from the knife of the midwife, consumed far too much wine. As the night moved along, Rachel was the only one who noticed Leah's sons were drinking very little. This abstinence was strange, as those men liked to drink. Not even Joseph, who had a keen eye for detail, noticed the abstinence. Occupied with two Hivite women, he did not notice Simeon and Levi leave the celebration. Caught up on the most joyous night of my life, I saw no one but Shekem. I was grateful that he had not overindulged, and so it was; we danced the night away. When the time came, Hamor had everyone stand, goblet in hand, and presented the Hivite marriage toast. Bursting with expectation, I liked that it was short.

He said, "May your life together be one of joy, and may you bring forth many healthy sons and daughters."

The guests responded in unison, "Sons and daughters."

Hamor nodded to Shekem, took a few steps, and waited for my husband to offer me his arm so that he might escort me to our new home. Hamor led the way, opened the door, and we entered. For a brief moment, I remembered mother telling me how intoxicated Jacob had been on their wedding night. I was thankful that Shekem had been so considerate.

This night is what a girl waits sixteen years to experience. I remembered that God had instructed our ancestors Adam and Eve to be fruitful and multiply. At that moment, I felt so very fruitful and was definitely ready to multiply. Everything about our preparation to enter the marriage bed was arousing and sensual. I had not considered myself naive, but on this night, my senses tingled with the expectation of the unknown. My gown dropped, I entered our bed, Shekem followed, took me in his arms, and kissed me. He was young, strong, and virile. The night was as mother and Rachel had said, and words could never describe the immense pleasure of shared lovemaking. This night, and the rest of our lives, was before us. I was in heaven.

Overwhelmed with the pleasures of our wedding bed, we were oblivious to the activity outside in the village. Simeon and Levi had organized their brothers, shepherds, and servants into pairs. One man carried a walking staff and the other a short sword. In the village courtyard, guests began returning to their homes. Rachel had to have a Hivite woman help her take Jacob to his tent in our encampment. She told me later that her heart grew heavy when she realized all the Hebrew men had left the courtyard but did not know why. Inside the bedroom, Shekem was tireless. Then, all hades broke loose. *Bang!* The door flew off its hinges. Levi charged in and began swinging his staff onto the back of my husband. Again and again, blow after blow turned indescribable pleasure into a nightmare. I rolled on top to protect my husband, but Levi grabbed me by the hair and pulled me onto the floor. At last, one powerful blow to the head and Shekem flew off the bed and onto the floor. Then, one final atrocity; Simeon descended upon my beloved and drove his sword into Shekem's heart.

While the surreal nightmare was screaming in my mind, Simeon stood. Shekem's eyes found mine. It was uncanny how his eyes were not full of pain but sadness, the sadness of losing me. All went silent. Shekem's lifeless body collapsed. A moment later, my screaming broke the silence. Simeon threw Levi Shekem's cloak. Levi covered me. Each took an arm and dragged me from my wedding chamber. In an instant, my heart turned from heavenly bliss to hatred. It felt as if my life had ended along with that of my beloved.

That morning, Jacob awoke to the clammer and commotion in the village. Shepherds herded sheep, oxen, goats, and donkeys through the village to the pasture land.

Only Hivite women and very young children had been left alive. My family had slaughtered a village of innocent men who only sought to be our friends and neighbors. Exiting his tent, Jacob stood in front of a cart loaded with all the valuables of Shalem. Simeon, still in his blood-soaked robe, spoke first.

"Look father, we have more than a dowry."

"Yes," added Levi, "we now have a village we can call our own."

"No more living in tents," Simeon announced with pride.

Jacob was genuinely dumbfounded. He couldn't speak. He just stood there for the longest time, trying to comprehend what had taken place. By this time, Rachel and Yowceph stood in horror beside Jacob. Unable to speak, Jacob turned, Rachel and Yowceph escorted him back into his tent.

Without the slightest inkling of wrongdoing, Simeon said to Levi "Come, let us divide the women and treasure."

Before he could move off, Yowceph stepped out of Jacob's tent and called to Hamor's wife. Yiskah, broke loose and ran into Jacob's tent.

Moments later, Yowceph yelled again, "Simeon, Levi, father wants to see you."

They entered to see Yiskah kneeling beside Jacob. His eyes filled with tears.

Simeon was quick to speak first, "Father, we did this because Shekem raped our sister."

Yiskah screamed, "My son did no such thing. He loved Dinah far too much."

Just then, I burst in screaming, "You bastard, you killed my husband so that you could steal his wealth! Look outside father. Look at what they have done!"

Levi went to speak, but Jacob put his hand up. Levi froze.

Eyes weeping, Jacob said, "You have made me a stink to the inhabitants of this land. The Canaanites and the Perizzites know we are few in number. We cannot stay in this land. The tribes shall gather themselves against me. I and my house shall be destroyed."

Simeon refusing to acknowledge his crime, replied, "Should he deal with our sister as a harlot?"

I screamed again, "I was a virgin on my wedding night. Shekem did no such thing. He was an honorable man."

I lunged at Simeon. My nails dug into his neck, but Levi was quick to pull me off.

Jacob shouted, "Go! Everyone go. Allow me to be alone with my God." As we left the tent, Jacob called to Yowceph.

When alone, he said, "Quickly, you must go to the surrounding villages and say that *Elelohe*, the mighty God of Israel, will defend Jacob against all who seek punishment for avenging the rape of his daughter in this way."

"But father," Yowceph began, "Dinah was not raped."

"They will not know. Go, lest we be destroyed like the people of Shalem."

Later that day, Jacob called the people together and said, "It is not safe for us to remain in this land. We will travel to Bethel, where our God first spoke with me. Be ready to move first thing in the morning." About to enter his tent, Jacob turned and called out so that the people harkened unto his voice again. He said, "Bring all your household idols and godly images to me this evening."

Rachel ordered the shepherds to help Yiskah and her people bury their dead. Shekem and Hamor were buried under the oak of Shalem, and a smaller grave was dug beside them. In the evening, all the idols and images were placed before Jacob. After dropping the idols into the smaller grave, two shepherds dumped the entrails of an old donkey onto the idols and then the carcass. The idols were covered over with dirt.

The following morning, they journeyed to Bethel. Jacob's ploy had worked. The terror of their God was upon the cities that were round about them, and they did not pursue after the sons of Jacob.

Chapter 5

Judah and Tamar

THE JOURNEY SOUTH was slow and, for the most part, sad. When the gravity of Simeon's actions settled in the minds of Jacob's people, a sense of guilt contributed to the silence. The horror of the slaughter, the journey south, and a difficult pregnancy became very stressful for Rachel. She was happy to be with child, but with the pain becoming more unbearable, Jacob made camp early. That evening, in a makeshift tent, we had no choice but to call upon Yiskah to be the midwife. I did not have a good feeling about Rachel. My emotions were so distraught, all I could do was watch. Yiskah was not Hebrew. Her midwifery skills were lacking. Rachel's pain increased as the moment of delivery grew near. She began screaming as never before.

Yiskah sat back and said, "I have never felt anything like this in the past. If I take the child, the mother will die; if I push the child back," Yiskah looked at me and continued, "the child is breached, and it will die."

Without a second thought, Rachel screamed, "Benyamin, save Benyamin!"

I cried, "No, save Rachel!"

It did not matter. Rachel collapsed. I sat in horror as I watched the life drain from my auntie's body Yiskah removed the child. Confusion, upset, crying, hysteria, all were a mess. Yiskah managed to cut the umbilical cord, and the other women cleaned Benyamin, a healthy baby boy. At sixteen years of age, Azrael, the angel of death, had taken my mother, my husband, and now my aunt from me. In the morning, servants strapped my aunt to a donkey. The same animal had carried her sister, my mother, to be with her ancestors. We journeyed to the cave at Machpelah. I watched as they placed Leah's bones beside those of Rebekah's, dusted the stone slab, and lay Rachel in her final place of rest. Father told me later that he wished he had died with her. I knew how he felt. Just days before, I had felt the same way. Our journey, like life, carried on.

Corralled in one location, Jacob's sons kept watch over the captive Hivite women throughout the night. The second day Rachel noticed Yiskah going from one woman to the next, offering her sympathies. The day's travel had been long and grueling through the hills. Mealtime was short with flatbread, cheese, and water. The Hivite women were corralled and guarded once again. Issachar and Zebulun took the first watch. The middle watch was taken by Naphtali and Dan, two of the younger brothers. During Yiskah's sympathetic visits, she had also been taking a count. Twelve women had multiple children and no place to go, even had they been set free. Two of those women volunteered to distract the watch. They snuggled up to Naphtali and Dan, uncovered their captor's feet, and provided a pleasant distraction. When Asher and Gad arrived to take the morning watch, they found their brothers asleep with their distractors.

Simeon knew it would be hopeless and a complete waste of time to take chase. He also knew that to divide the men would leave them vulnerable. The older women with older children had escaped, but that was okay. The younger women would be more desirable as wives, and their children were too young to remember the atrocity. To speed up the journey, the sons each took a wife. Naphtali and Dan were happy to take the women they had spent the night. With the need to watch corralled captives eliminated, the trek took a little over three weeks. Arriving at the place Jacob had spent the night so many years ago, he was happy to find the rock he had set up to mark the place he called Bethel.

Taking a handful of wheat, he let it fall over the rock. Knowing Rueben and Judah had no part in the slaughter, Rueben poured olive oil over the stone, and Judah poured wine. The encampment did not take long to look like it had been there for a long time. When Jacob was happy, he ordered a lamb and a goat to be slain. Their entrails were offered as a sacrifice in the central fire pit, and the carcasses roasted. Jacob commanded every man who took part in the slaughter at Shalem to write *ratsach* (murderer) on a piece of goatskin and pin it to a lamb without blemish so that the pin drew blood. When all had finished, Jacob prayed and slapped the lamb so that it ran off into the wilderness. It was uncanny to listen to the cries as wolves smelled the scent of blood and devoured the screeching sacrificial animal.

Jacob prayed, "Almighty God, by the sacrifice of this pure white lamb, forgive the sins of my sons this day, this Yom Kippur."

I thought to myself, "*God may forgive, but I will not.*"

***

Jacob and his sons thought it best to keep to themselves as the atrocity was still fresh in the people's minds in the region. The stories of the mighty God of Israel had achieved their desired effect; the surrounding tribes kept to themselves. This avoidance meant that all trading took place in Yafa as Lebownah was too far north to make trading worthwhile. The year was uneventful, but the fear of reprisal had made it so Israel dared not trade in Jerusalem or Bethlehem. Rueben had spoken with his father and suggested that he try and marry me off to Esau's son Reuel. Everyone thought it a good idea; everyone except me. The discussion was hot and lively. Finally, I stood in front of Simeon, glaring into his eyes.

I said, "I'll scratch Reuel's eyes out on our wedding bed, and then we'll see what Ishmael does to you, my brother." Then I spit in Simeon's face.

Everyone was in shock. None of my brothers dared speak. Jacob told me to leave.

I cannot describe the feeling of loneliness that had come over me—first, my mother, then my husband, and now my aunt. With only one friend in the whole world, I resolved to raise Benyamin as my own. My family, however, disagreed, and when Levi came to take Benyamin away, I scratched his face so deep it took weeks to heal. That ended the discussion. Allowing Benyamin to suck, I soon was able to produce enough milk to feed this hungry baby boy. He grew strong and healthy, bringing joy to my heart while watching him wobble about the village. I must confess, if there is one thing that can heal a broken heart, it is the love of a child. As the days passed, Benjamin continued to brighten my spirit, and I began to believe the pain of loss would never strike again. I was wrong.

Unaware of his sons' jealousy of Yowceph, Jacob purchased a special cloak from a merchant in a passing caravan. It was the most beautiful, most colorful cloak anyone had ever seen. Jacob made another mistake by presenting the cloak in the presence of his older brothers. This gift incited their jealousy even further. Yowceph, proud of his increasing ability to dream and interpret dreams though he might get even for all the abuse he had suffered over the years. He made the mistake of telling his brothers of a recent dream. He told them how they were all binding sheaves of wheat in the field and how his sheaf stood up. When it did, his brothers' sheaves stood and bowed to his sheaf. The telling of this dream was not the wisest thing Yowceph ever did. To make matters worse, later that week, Jacob sent Yowceph to check on his sons and report to him the state of his several flocks.

The sons of Zilpah, Asher, and Gad, and the sons of Bilhah, Naphtali, and Dan, had not bothered to remove fallen willow branches from the stream that watered their flock. As a result, many ewe lambs were no longer white but speckled. This imperfection meant a drop in the price of their fleece. On his return, Yowceph gave a bad report to Jacob, who chastised the boys for their neglect. The other sons decided "When Yowceph comes to Dothan to inspect our flock, we will kill him." Thankfully, Reuben stepped into the conversation and ended the plot. The others were determined. When Yowceph came the next week to inspect their flock, my brothers took hold of him and threw him in a pit until they could come up with a way to dispose of him. A caravan headed for Egypt passed close by the next day, so Jacob's sons sold Yowceph to the traveling slavers. Years earlier, Leah told me that Jacob's God works in mysterious ways and that God's ways are not our ways.

I asked, "Does God have people commit evil?"

"No," was her reply, "when people commit evil, God works to set another plan in place."

As if the selling of Yowceph into slavery wasn't enough to make me question God's ways, what I am about to tell you next was utterly beyond my comprehension.

Rueben was distressed when he returned to find Yowceph sold into slavery. After the family had fled Shalem, Jacob had assured Rueben that the blessing of birthright would pass to him. However, the other brothers had enough of the favoritism, and the bad report on Gad and Asher was the last straw. But now, Rueben needed a story to explain Yowceph's disappearance. He had Levi fetch Yowceph's colorful cloak from the pit. It was dirty. "*Good*," he thought.

Taking a knife, he ripped and slashed the garment. Gad killed a goat and let the blood pool. Reuben soaked the cloak in the goat's blood and then took it to his father. Broken-hearted, he explained to Jacob that his son had been set upon and devoured by wild animals. All that was left was the cloak. It was unmistakable. Jacob was distraught, as could be imagined.

Prior to Yowceph's sale to slavers, Judah, still disgusted with his brothers' actions in Shalem, set out on his own. Taking his flocks and servants, he headed north to Timnath. Going in unto Chiyrah, an older Adullamite woman he loved to frequent, Judah stayed with her until he had found suitable pasture to purchase. While there, he met Shuah, a healthy young Canaanite woman. They married, moved to his newly purchased land, prospered, and had two healthy boys. The eldest was named Er, and the younger Onan. Many years passed, and Shuah bore unto Judah another son named Shelah. That same year, Er married a tall and stately but naïve young woman named Tamar. Judah's prosperity and wealth had turned Er's mind to evil ways. His ways became so wicked and perverse; some say that it was God who killed him. Be that what it may, Er died without an heir. Exercising her right, Tamar went to Judah and requested the right of a kinsman. Judah instructed his son Oran to go in unto his brother's wife so that she would conceive a child. Oran was happy to have another woman uncover his feet but spilled his seed onto the ground each time he went in unto her. In this way, Tamar would never bear a son to claim the inheritance, and all would be his when Judah died.

This practice is where you need to understand our customs. Er was the rightful heir of Judah's wealth, which would necessarily pass to Er's son. In order to keep from being cast out or simply ending up with nothing and having to resort to prostitution or the lesser evil of becoming a concubine, Tamar needed a male child. Knowing what Oran was doing and why, Tamar went to Judah to complain. Judah's solution was, wait sixteen years until Shelah was old enough to impregnate her. That was not going to happen. I am so proud of Tamar for taking her destiny into her own hands. Shearing season was near, and she knew Judah would travel north and stay with his bed friend, Chiyrah.

Paying a local madame a rental fee, Tamar took a room in her brothel. After explaining her predicament, the madame gave Tamar a very revealing see-through garment and jeweled veil. Hiding behind the brothel doorway, she waited for Judah to pass by. When he did, it wasn't difficult to capture his attention. When Judah stopped to enjoy the view, Tamar spread her arms and danced around Judah, pressing her almost bare breasts against him. This erotic dance had its desired effect. Judah became so aroused he forgot that he had not planned on any expenditures. Taking his hand, she led him into the brothel and uncovered his feet. The afternoon of pleasure over, Judah found himself without silver. Tamar called the madame, and the two women made him offer a pledge. Unaware the prostitute was his daughter-in-law, he offered his signet ring and bracelet, promising to return shortly with a female goat. Judah must have enjoyed himself immensely as a goat, especially a female goat for milking, was of very high value. Returning a short while later, the madame reported that the young woman left immediately following his departure, and she did not know where the prostitute had gone.

It came to pass that four months later, Judah found that his daughter-in-law Tamar had played the harlot and was with child by whoredom. This bias is one of the things about our culture that still bothers me. It is perfectly acceptable for the man to bed whoever and however many women he desires. This same conduct means death for the woman. Allow me to illustrate.

When Tamar was brought before her father-in-law, she carried a towel in her hand.

Judah looked upon her in disgust and said, "Let her be burnt to death."

Curious as to why Tamar would hold so tightly to the towel, he asked, "What is that in your hand?"

Slowly unwrapping the towel, she said, "These are the pledge from the man that gave me this child." When revealed, she held them out and continued, "Tell me, my father-in-law, whose are these signet and bracelet?"

Trapped before family and friends, Judah admitted that he was the father. This admission meant that the blessing and birthright would legally pass to her child if it were male.

Judah acknowledged that Tamar had been more righteous than he; because he did not make Oran give her a son.

When the time of her delivery came, the midwife reported that it was the strangest birth she had ever seen. Apparently, a hand appeared first. The midwife took a crimson ribbon from her hair and tied it on the wrist. Then, as mysteriously as it had appeared, it disappeared, and another child, a baby boy, was birthed in the usual manner. Immediately thereafter, the baby boy with the crimson ribbon on his wrist was birthed. The second child was named Pharez. The child whose hand broke forth from the womb first was named Zarah.

Remember how I had said that God works in mysterious ways? Well, when best-laid plans seem thwarted, God simply devises another plan. God had chosen Abraham and the Hebrew people to be a holy nation. Not just to have a holy nation, but to demonstrate to all creation what life could be like if they stopped worshipping false gods and acknowledged the one true living God. After years of barrenness, Sarah gave birth to Isaac. The first problem was solved.

When Isaac stopped listening, Rebekah was the one God spoke with to secure the birthright for Jacob. The second problem was solved. When Jacob did not return with a wife, God had to prosper him to become a tribal leader. The third problem was solved.

But now, Judah had left the fold, and Yowceph was sold into Egyptian slavery at seventeen years of age. Life did not go well for Yowceph, and he ended up in prison. Thirteen years later, Yowceph interpreted Pharaoh's dream of impending famine and ended up as regent over Egypt. When the famine devastated Jacob's world, he sent his sons to Egypt to buy wheat. By this act, Jacob and many other tribes from the region migrated to Egypt to wait out the famine. Life was good. Pasture and water were plentiful. Work in the quarries and servanthood in the wealthy homes caused the Hebrew people and many other tribes to remain. Yowceph had two sons, and the now acceptable inter-tribal marriage caused the numbers to explode. Hundreds of years later, the Hyksos invaded lower Egypt and remained in power for over one hundred years, before Northern Egypt, under Pharaoh Ahmose I, drove them out. Fearing the Semitic people might side with the Hyksos, should they decide to re-invade, Pharaoh Ahmose corralled all foreign people into Goshen. With their freedom suddenly gone, tens of thousands of Semitic people found themselves working as slaves. The fourth problem was solved.

God needed a deliverer. Moshe was born, but at forty years of age, he killed an Egyptian and ran away to Midian, a descendant of Ishmael. At eighty years of age, God called him to return to Egypt and lead the Semitic people to freedom. Through deceit and after more than one hundred years of harsh slavery, this mass of people fled Pharaoh. That story is for another time. Sadly, after everything God had done for the people of Israel, they were still determined to worship false gods. In disgust and anger, God caused the earth to part and consume many of the people. Their faithlessness does not end there.

When God led the people to the Promised Land, the land promised to Abraham hundreds of years earlier; their faithlessness surfaced once again. When those sent to spy out the land reported how Nephilim(giants) made them feel like grasshoppers, the people cried out in fear that they wanted to go back to Egypt. As punishment for their continual lack of faith and trust in the LORD, the people were sentenced to wander in the wilderness until every faithless adult male had died. The spies had spent forty days searching out the Promised Land. The punishment was one year of wandering in the wilderness for every day the spies spent in the land. At the time, a child would have been considered an adult at about fifteen years of age. This information means that male longevity was fifty-five years of age.

As you can see, at every interval of disruption, God called men and women to fulfill the promise to Abraham. Should you ever be interested to hear of the Exodus, my friends, the ghosts of Amram, Moshe's father, and Miryam, Moshe's sister, will be happy to tell you their story. However, I will tell you that many years after Israel entered the Promised Land, both men and women were called upon to judge the people's rights and wrongs. One such Judge was named Samson. Following his crushing death, he was laid to rest with his ancestors. I have asked the ghost of the woman whom men say, "Led poor Samson astray," to tell you the story of his fateful demise.

Chapter 6

Samson

SAMSON'S STORY BEGINS WITH the angel of the LORD coming to a man named Manoah. As often happened, divinely inspired births frequently occurred among barren women. As it came to pass, Manoah's wife, Hazzelelponi, bore unto him a fine healthy boy they named Samson (like the sun). He was named Samson because his hair was golden blonde and blonde hair was even rarer than red hair. The angel of the LORD had stipulated the child was to be raised as a Nazarite. The requirements of a Nazarite are stringent. They must vow to separate themselves from a common association with others, dedicate their lives to the LORD, and never partake of strong drinks or wine. They were even forbidden to eat grapes, moist or dried, all the days of their lives. Please remember these requirements as you hear the story of Samson, a judge in Israel.

As he grew, the LORD blessed him. His golden hair grew long, and the longer it grew, the stronger he became. As a Nazarene, Samson was forbidden to have it cut. However, Samson did not take to separating himself from the common folk. One of the reasons was, he liked to fight and was good at it. When old enough, he began to chase women and drink strong drinks. He liked these vices even more than fighting. Not long after being introduced to the erotic pleasures of women, Samson heard that many of the daughters of the Philistines were liberal with their special favors, so he decided to go down to Timnath and check them out. After that experience, and still young and impressionable, he told his father to get a particular woman to be his wife. Manoah and Hazzelelponi were upset that he would consider taking a wife from the uncircumcised Philistines but did as requested. On one trip to visit his wife-to-be, Samson came across a lion. When the lion attacked, he broke its neck as easily as if it had been a kid goat. Samson made many trips to Timnath as the woman pleased him well.

Nearing the wedding day, Samson traveled to Timnath for another conjugal visit. When he passed the lion's carcass, he noticed bees had built a hive in the rib cavity. On his return trip, he took honeycombs from the hive and gave them to his parents but did not say where or how he came upon them. Later Manoah went to the woman's parents and arranged a feast to celebrate the forthcoming wedding. Friends and relatives were invited. On hearing of the feast, thirty young Philistines were bold enough to invite themselves. Samson did not get mad. He propositioned the young men by saying that he would supply each man a garment if anyone could answer his riddle correctly. The catch was, if they could not, each man had to give him a garment. The men agreed.

Samson said, "Out of the eater came forth meat, and out of the strong came forth sweet. After three days, they could not explain the riddle. Frustrated and perplexed, the men put pressure on Samson's wife. They threatened to burn her father's house, with them in it, if she did not persuade her husband to declare the riddle's answer.

Samson's wife wept before him and said, "You must hate me and must not love me because you refuse to tell me the answer to your riddle."

Samson replied, "I have not told the answer to my father nor my mother. Shall I now reveal it to you?

Enduring the constant badgering for as long as he could, Samson broke down and told his wife the answer. She immediately ran to the men and told them the riddle's answer.

Just before sundown on the final day, all thirty men came to Samson and said, "What is stronger than a lion, and what is sweeter than honey?"

Realizing the deceit, Samson said, "If you had not plowed with my heifer, you would not have found the answer to my riddle."

Angered by the conspiracy, Samson went down to Ashkelon, slew thirty Philistines, stripped their garments and gave them to the thirty Philistines who answered the riddle.

Unable to speak knowledgeably about the marriage customs of the Philistines, it seems strange to me that after the seven days of wedding celebrations, Samson returned to his father's home. When the wheat harvest came, Samson returned to his wife but found she was at her father's house. Wanting to enter the bed-chamber to lay with his wife, Samson learned that the father had given his wife to a man Samson thought was his friend. Frightened by his anger, the father said Samson could have his younger daughter, saying, "She is much more beautiful and not as chubby."

Samson went and caught foxes, turned tail to tail, bound the tails, and tied a torch to them. Taking the foxes to the cornfield, he lit the torches and set the foxes running. What he had not anticipated was the foxes did not stop there. The torches continued to burn, and the foxes continued to run, setting the fields of wheat, vineyards, and olive groves ablaze. The Philistines were furious, and when they discovered who had done this and why, they came to her father's house and set it ablaze, with the family inside. It must be remembered that the Hebrews were living in the land of the Philistines.

Nonetheless, when Samson learned of their retaliation, he marched to the village to avenge his father-in-law's death by physically beating every man to death. Not that you will be surprised, but the Philistines sought revenge upon him for the great slaughter. For over three thousand years, this thirst for blood lust revenge has been the way of life for people in the land of Canaan. Sometimes, retaliation took place four and five generations later. Time did not matter. Semitic people never forget a transgression. So it was, the Philistine army went up to Lehi to do battle with the tribe of Judah. Judah's three thousand men went up to the rock at Etam, where Samson was known to recline and rest. Samson asked the commander why he had come up against him.

The commander replied, "Do you not know the Philistines are rulers over us? Why have you done such a thing?"

Samson replied, "As they have done unto me, so have I done unto them."

The commander said, "We have no choice. We are here to bind and deliver into the hand of the Philistines so that we may not have to go to war."

Appreciating the commander's honesty, Samson said, "Swear unto me, that *you* will do me no harm, and you may bind me."

The commander gave Samson his word, bound him with a new rope, and took him to the Philistines assembled at Lehi. The commander turned Samson around to demonstrate that they had bound his wrists with a new rope. Then Samson was placed into the clutches of two Philistine soldiers. Taking Samson away, the soldiers made a big mistake. Observing the skeleton of a donkey off to the side of the path, the soldiers pushed Samson onto the skeleton. Thinking it was funny, they made crude remarks about his mother. Samson turned so that all the soldiers could see the rope that bound his wrists was tied tight. With a little yank, the rope snapped. Samson kicked the donkey's head, picked up the jawbone, smacked it against his other hand, and said, "You should not have insulted my mother."

Samson swung the jawbone twice. The soldiers each lost their jawbone. The remainder of the troop stood in horror as Samson walked toward them, tapping the jawbone of the ass on his hand. The scene looked like a day at the theatre. Three thousand Hebrew soldiers sat around the crest of a hill. They watched as Samson put to death Philistine after Philistine in the valley below. As the bodies piled up, Samson would move and make another pile. Having positioned himself so that he could not be surrounded, Samson spent most of the afternoon beating Philistine soldiers to death. Many became frightened and ran off. Samson called the place *Ramathlehi* because he killed one thousand Philistines there.

Thirsting beyond belief, Samson called upon the LORD, saying, "You have given your servant a great victory this day. Now, am I to die of thirst so that I should perish before these uncircumcised Philistines?" Samson looked to the place where the donkey skeleton had lain, and a spring of water burst forth. His thirst satisfied, and his spirit revived; Samson named the place *Enhakkore*.

Traveling to Gaza, Samson entered an inn to order his favorite lamb chops marinated in wine and salt with a seasoning of rosemary and mint along with a pitcher of heqet (beer). Satisfied, he asked the innkeeper if Liora was still here. He was told Liora was in the room marked with a lamed. Thinking to himself, "*How blessed am I; a good fight; good food and drink, and now my favorite prostitute. Life doesn't get any better."*

And so, Samson went in unto his favorite prostitute. Now the men of Gaza knew the reason Samson had come to the inn. They gathered and set a plan knowing Samson always spent the night. Closing the city gate, wrapping it with a chain, they agreed to gather outside the gate before sunrise and went to their homes. However, this night, Samson had a vision and decided to leave after midnight. Finding the gate chained, he ripped the posts out of the ground, folded the gate one over the other, put it upon his shoulders, and carried it away. The next day, he placed the gates atop the hill overlooking Hebron. The Philistines were outraged.

At this point in my story, I have asked the woman who seduced the mighty Samson to his demise to tell her story. Delilah is her name. She was a Philistine prostitute, but that matters no longer as all ghosts on the shephelah are equal. Please do not be misled, as her name in Hebrew means feeble. Let me tell you; her name does not mean feeble in the Philistine language. She was beautiful, and her body was designed for one thing; pleasing men. Be pleased to hear firsthand the demise of Samson as told by the seductress, Delilah.

The Grand Seduction

The week passed with no reprisal from the Philistines, so Samson, feeling aroused again, decided to visit me, the new woman who had recently moved to Timnath in the Sorek Valley. He told me on one of his previous visits that I was the most amazing prostitute he'd even lain. Not to brag, but my amorous charms seduced Samson with little effort. So much so, he fell in love. My name is Delilah and I am a Philistine. As you can imagine, nothing gets past prying eyes in a small village. So it was, three lords of the Philistines heard of Samson's beguilement and came offering a bribe. Each man pledged to pay me eleven hundred pieces of silver if I could discover the source of his great strength. After Samson lay with me that evening, servants brought him strong drink, which he enjoyed. Stroking his chest, I asked, "Tell me; I pray thee, wherein lies the source of your great strength, my big strong hunk of handsome Hebrew?"

Accustomed to people wanting to know, he said, "If you bind me with seven fresh green reeds, then shall I be as weak as any other man. Servants were sent and returned a short while later with seven green reeds.

Samson said, "Now weave them into a rope and bind my wrists."

The servants did so, and I bound his wrist. One of my female servants raised a cup of wine to Samson's lips.

At that moment, I yelled, "The Philistines be upon thee, Samson."

Samson jumped up, spilled the wine, snapped the reeds as if they were a single thread.

With fake tears of sadness, I said, "You mock me Samson. If you love me as you say, you will not mock me this time. Now tell me, please, how can I bind you?"

Samson hesitated but then said, "Bind my wrists with a new rope, and I shall become weak. When the servant returned with the rope, I pulled his hands behind his back, made three wraps, and tied the rope.

Kissing his neck from behind, I suddenly pushed him forward and screamed, "The Philistines be upon thee, Samson!"

Regaining his balance, Samson snapped the ropes and readied himself. I feigned sadness once again—a tear rand down my cheek.

I sat and pouted, saying, "You have mocked me again with your lies, now tell me please, how may I bind you."

"Wine, more wine, and let us stop these childish games," he said.

The servants continued to serve more wine, and I continued to caress his muscular body until Samson said, "Weave my hair into seven locks. Then take new flax from the loom, weave the locks into one and wrap the locks with the flax. Roll the lock into a ball and pin."

All the while, Samson continued to drink, and let me tell you, he could outdrink any man I ever knew. When the servants had finished, he lay down and slept. Confident he had not lied to me a third time, I sent for the Philistine soldiers in wait.

As the soldiers rushed in, I shouted, "The Philistines be upon you Samson."

Two soldiers jumped upon him. Samson broke the neck of the first soldier, broke the back of the second, and the rest ran out as quickly as possible.

This time, visibly agitated, sobbing and crying, I began again, "How can you say you love me when your heart is not truthful? You have mocked me these three times and not told me wherein the source of your great strength."

Enduring what he called "This foolishness" long enough, Samson got up and left.

Each time Samson came to visit, I pressed him, but he would not reveal the source of his strength. Knowing if I kept badgering him, he would find another woman, and the reward would be lost and possibly my life. After devising an all-out plan, I arranged for three very charming young and beautiful prostitutes to assist me. That afternoon servants marinated three racks of lamb. Other servants arranged on a table, among the fruit and bread, an abundant supply of wine and liquor. When Samson arrived for his conjugal visit, he was greeted by the three scantily clad young women. Each had a different colored transparent scarf draped over her shoulders, with another scarf tied around the waist. The tail ends falling between their legs.

The young girls began serving Samson wine. Feeling like a king, he reached up and pulled the shoulder scarf from one of the girls. This game delighted him beyond measure. Each time a different girl refreshed his wine, Samson removed her shoulder scarf. I instructed the girls to sway their shoulders each time he removed their scarf. The girls were to allow their attributes to brush Samson's face. Temporarily forgetting whom he had come to see, I reminded him on entering, dressed identical to the girls, carrying a tray of roasted lamb chops and green vegetables. I knelt between his legs holding the tray. Never had Samson enjoyed his ribs so much. The half-naked girls took turns feeding him. During his titillating feeding frenzy, Samson had not noticed servants replacing the wine with liquor. Lost is the most erotic evening of his life; Samson found himself in bed with four naked women.

While the girls kissed and caressed him, I continued to whisper in his ear, "Samson, the source of your strength. Samson, do you not remember, you promised to tell me."

Over and over again, I whispered those soft, seductive words. Delirious with pleasure, Samson raised his hands and ran his fingers through his long golden hair.

His body, tingling as never before, he moaned softly, "My hair. It is my hair."

Puzzled, I asked, "Your hair?"

From birth, I have been a Nazarite, and my hair has never been cut."

This time, I knew I had finally succeeded. The girls continued pleasuring Samson until he collapsed and fell into a deep sleep. The time had come. Not wanting to take any chances, I had the girls cut his beautiful long golden hair and rub lotion onto his head. Taking a razor, I shaved his head smooth. A servant was sent to bring the Philistines lords to my house. Fifty armed soldiers arrived with the three lords who had promised me the silver reward. A few brave soldiers surround Samson. I shook his head until he began to awaken from his drunken stupor.

Then I shouted, "The Philistines be upon thee, Samson."

Opening his eyes, he found himself being hauled to his feet. Attempting to break free, nothing happened. One of the lords stepped forward and slapped Samson's face. He struggled but to no avail. He could not break the soldier's grip. The second lord removed a knife from his sash and plunged it into Samson's eye. The third lord did the same to the other eye. Blood trickled down his cheeks. One of the girls vomited.

Satisfied that I had found the source of Samson's strength, the first lord said, "Your chest of silver will arrive in the morning."

I was actually saddened that I would no longer enjoy the pleasure he provided but delighted to receive the silver; after all, I was a prostitute.

The Philistines took Samson, bound in fetters of brass, to Gaza, where they cast him into prison. They were at least gracious enough to allow a few weeks for his eyes to heal over. A skilled craftsman cut and polished two pieces of Carrera marble. These white and black stones were then fit into Samson's eye sockets. In an instant, life had changed for Samson. Now completely blind, his time in prison gave him cause to reflect how he had never embraced the life of a Nazarene and squandered God's gift on carnal pleasures. With the festival to Dagon still six full moons away, the Philistine lords decided to heap an even greater insult upon their captive. Years ago, a grist mill was built in their prison so criminals could grind wheat grain into flour. The lords decided to hitch Samson to the grinding stone so that he would spend the remainder of his days in disgrace, plodding in a circle, grinding wheat.

Difficult at first, as the days and weeks passed, he found the shaft easier to push. The Philistines were so occupied hurling insults through the prison gates they failed to see that Samson became at ease in his daily march. While the people were shouting praises unto Dagon, Samson humbled himself to pray unto the LORD his God. The days passed. Strength replaced agony. Sweat-covered chest muscles glistened in the sun. Forgetting that the source of Samson's strength was his golden hair, no one paid attention to its growth. The day of celebration drew near. Philistines from near and far journeyed to Gaza. For three days, people hurled insults through the prison gates. Finally, the day arrived, the celebration began. The central area of the temple courtyard had been cleared for the spectacle. In actual fact, it was more like an arena used for worship and sacrifice.

On that day, a once-popular performance took place in memory of their ancient Minoan ancestors. Four massive bulls were brought into the temple courtyard. It took five days for dozens of men to bring the stone image of Dagon to the temple and raise it on top of the two main pillars. Samson was brought to the temple and chained between those two main pillars. It was a sight to behold; Samson chained to pillars supporting the stone image of Dagon above his head. The celebration was to end with Samson, spread eagle on his back, in the middle of the courtyard. Chains were to have been attached to his wrists and ankles and then fastened to four bulls. The ceremony would culminate with their long-time enemy being torn apart by the bulls.

The festivities began. A dozen athletes, men and women, clothed in only loincloths, paraded into the arena. A bull was released, and the bull jumping began. Athlete and bull faced each other. The bull charged, the athlete charged. A moment before the fateful collision, the athlete dove into the air, landed with both hands on the bull's shoulders, and performed a majestic somersault over, landing perfectly balanced. The ancient event was an amazing display of grace and timing. It was one thing to see a man leap into the air in front of a charging bull, but it was even more interesting to watch women do the same thing just as gracefully. When the athletes landed, judges held up scorecards, the audience cheered. Sad to say, but part of the attraction was that not every bull jumper survived. After facing three contestants, one of the bulls stopped precisely at the right time. Not for the jumper. For the bull. The athlete found himself landing with his back onto the bull's horns. The audience cheered for the bull. Some moaned as the bull flung the man against the stone wall of the courtyard. His body fell lifeless to the ground.

With the afternoon's fun spectacle over, the athletes lined up, and a judge selected two winners. One man and one woman were escorted to the center of the temple courtyard, and the judge held up both of their hands. The audience cheered wildly.

Anxious to see the demise of their enemy, three thousand Philistines had crowded into the courtyard. All the seats were full. Brave ones sat on the top of the court walls. Four bulls, each with four men holding a leash, were led into the arena. Samson could sense the anticipation. An adventurous young lad snuck in close to Samson and told him what was happening.

Crouching on one knee, Samson asked, "Please put my hands on the center of these columns. I wish to pray."

The lad, not realizing to whom Samson wished to pray, placed his hands on the pillars.

Samson began in a soft voice, "O LORD God, remember and strengthen me, I pray thee this one last time that I may be avenged for my two eyes." Using the muscles in his legs in unison with his arms and shoulders, Samson rose, pushing with all his might. Raising his voice as loud as possible, he shouted, "Let me die with these uncircumcised Philistines!"

Samson gave one last mighty push, and the house fell. People on top of the walls screamed as they fell upon those in their seats. Dagon got his revenge crushing Samson. Samson got his revenge as the stones destroyed all the lords and the people in the temple. The dead he slew that day were more than all he slew in his life. When word of the disaster reached his brethren, they came and took his body and buried him between Zorah and Eshtaol in the burying place of Manoah, his father. I did not attend as I wanted to remember my loverboy as the strongest, virile, golden-haired sex machine I'd ever had the delight of pleasing.

***

I am grateful for the ghost of Delilah's to tell of Samson's demise; now, allow me to continue my narration. Men have always told the story of a prince who lost his life because he raped a young Hebrew virgin. The only thing they were right about was that I was a virgin, and I need to say that I remained a virgin unto my marriage night. Shekem was an honorable man, and he wanted to marry the woman he loved; me, Dinah, the daughter of Jacob.

They say that Samson judged Israel twenty years. The problem with that is, I do not know of one judgment he was asked to make. As in the story of my so-called rape, male bias has a way of shaping a story. I was in love with the one man who had come into my life, and they labeled me a whore. Samson went in unto whores all his life, and they honored him as a judge. They said, "Shekem took (*laqach*) me by force. If that is so, the word *laqach* must necessarily keep the same meaning each time a man *takes* a woman. The problem is, *laqach* does not imply force, as you can see below.

Abraham *laqach* Sarah as wife;

Isaac *laqach* Rebekah as wife;

Jacob *laqach* Leah and Rachel as wives.

Now, look at the words in the story of Amnon, who forced/raped (*anah*) his stepsister.

Amnon was stronger than Tamar, forcing (*anah*) her to lay (*shakab*) with him.

You can see that the Hebrew language is precise, and words clearly define the action.

Samson was the story of a man who, if nothing else, was a constant nemesis to the Philistines, the undying enemy of the Hebrew people. To Israeli men, Samson is a hero. To Israeli women, their hero is Hadassah. You may know her as Esther. From the time Judah's tribe was in Babylonian exile, Hebrew women have passed her story down throughout the ages. Now, it is my delight to pass it on to you.

Chapter 7

Esther

KING AHASUERUS RULED the Persian empire from his palace in Shushan. The empire was said to have stretched from India to Ethiopia. He was a gracious man, but like all men, especially kings, he demanded respect, especially from women. His palace was spectacular, with green and blue banners hanging on fine linen cords attached to silver rings. The pavement throughout was a magnificent display of red, blue, white, and black marble. Majestic white Carrera pillars stood upon bases of gold and silver. Gold drinking vessels, filled with the very best wines, adorned the tables of every banquet. Shushan was known in the ancient world for its abundance of lilies. His harem, filled with women of every color and race, was the envy of the ancient world. Within the harem, there was one exceptionally beautiful woman named Vashti. So enamored by her beauty, Ahasuerus appointed her queen. Parading his trophy wife before the princes of the empire stroked the king's vanity.

Banquets in the realm were frequent. Ahasuerus was fond of displaying and sharing his wealth with the princes of Persia and Media. A Prince of Persia asked if Ahasuerus might delight his guests by presenting Vashti, his most beautiful queen, during the evening's banquet. Happily acquiescing to the request, the king sent his chamberlain to summon his queen to attend the banquet.

Slighted that she and the wives of the princes had not been invited, Vashti held a feast of her own and ignored the request. Not only was it the wrong decision, it was also costly.

Ahasuerus consulted with his advisor Memucan. They agreed that disrespecting a king in front of princes and foreign guests was unforgivable. Everyone agreed that allowing a queen to disobey a king would set a bad example. If tolerated, then women everywhere might start to disobey their husbands. Memucan was ordered to prepare a decree and publish it throughout the empire. The decree stated that Vashti would never come before the king again as punishment for disobeying her husband. She lost her royal position as queen and was cast out of the harem into a life of poverty. This punishment served as an example to all women that every man should bear rule over his own house.

Perplexed, Ahasuerus asked, "What now shall I do for a trophy wife?"

Memucan, male chauvinism shining, suggested, "In your royal wisdom, send forth a decree throughout all one hundred and twenty-seven provinces of the empire. Require every province to select the most beautiful virgin within its borders. Then, the most beautiful virgins from within the kingdom will assemble at your palace in Shushan. There, they will be given into the care of Hegai, keeper of the women, for a time of purification. During this time, the princes who desire to participate will select thirty-three of the most beautiful women in the empire."

The princes shouted "Yeah," in agreement with Memucan's plan.

Looking to the princes. "From the thirty-three, they will select twelve to present to you."

The princes applauded excitedly.

"Am I to have multiple queens?" inquired Ahasuerus anxiously.

"No, my king," was Memucan's reply. "you will have the twelve virgins parade before you, one at a time so that you might inspect their individual beauty and then choose." Sitting back to ponder, the king looked at the smiling faces of his princes and nobility.

Memucan continued, "If you like, we will hold another banquet, and the princes can help you judge the twelve most beautiful women in the empire."

"Yes!" the princes responded, pleased at the idea of a beauty contest.

"But twelve wives Memucan?"

The princes shouted, "Yes, yes. We will choose the twelve most beautiful O great king."

The king pondered for a moment and then decreed, "I will put eleven in my harem and take the most beautiful virgin to be my queen."

"Yes," Memucan replied. "and I will arrange for a most extravagant banquet."

Ahasuerus thought this was a splendid idea and instructed Memucan to draft the decree.

***

Outside the gate of the royal palace, an elderly Jew by the name of Mordecai sat day after day awaiting an audience with the king. Rumors had begun to surface that influential Persians were jealous that Jews were filling many government positions. Concerned for the wellbeing of his people, Mordecai sought an audience with the king to plea for their safety. He had been taken into captivity with Jeconiah, the last king of Judah many years ago by Nebuchadnezzar. During the trek from Jerusalem to Babylon, Mordecai's younger brother Abihail and wife died. He adopted their only child Hadassah and raised her as his own. Shortly after heralds announced the search for a new queen, Mordecai knew they would come for his Hadassah. She was extremely beautiful and a virgin.

"Mordecai cautioned her, saying, "When they come for you, my child, you will say that your name is Esther."

"But why father, my name is Hadassah?"

You are Hadassah, and our enemies will seek to destroy you because you are a Jew."

"But why would anyone want to hurt us. We are a peaceful people."

"Prejudice my daughter, prejudice. At this very moment, influential people in high places seek to destroy our people. That is why I cannot gain an audience with the king as each attempt is blocked. You must somehow gain the confidence of the king and speak on our behalf to keep the Jewish people from destruction."

"I understand and will do my best. From this day forth, I shall be known as Esther."

"And may our God watch over and protect you."

It was as Mordecai had said. Known for her beauty, Esther was selected.

One hundred and twenty-seven most beautiful virgins in the kingdom were selected and brought to Babylon. Knowing how to stroke the ego of his princes, Ahasuerus asked them to pick the twelve most beautiful virgins from the one hundred and twenty-seven. As a reward, each prince that volunteered would be allowed to take one of the unselected virgins into his home. Esther and eleven other girls were chosen and put in the care of Hegai. For two full moons, the young girls were bathed, massaged with oil of myrrh, and purified with all manner of exotic spices. Then came the time for each girl to parade before the king and his court. When Esther's turn came, she did as Mordecai had instructed. Her hair was braided in the manner of wealthy Persian women. She instructed her attendants to perfume her neck and hips very lightly. After stepping into golden slippers, an attendant draped her naked body with a pale green Dhaka muslin fabric. Although still a virgin, this was not the time for modesty. One by one, the young girls were led out to do their dance before the king. Esther thought, "*If I am to be noticed more than the others, I must do something different.*"

Anxious to be chosen, the other girls had danced before the king, boldly displaying their attributes. Then it occurred to Esther that she must start her dance self-conscious and timid. Esther had seven attendants surround her. This entrance surprised the princes in court. They strained to see the pearl encased by such a stunning shell. One by one, the attendants peeled away. Esther danced and spun, revealing only glimpses of herself first to the princes as she danced majestically around the hall. Then, she stopped abruptly before the king and spread her arms to the side. This gesture exposed her magnificent body through the Dhaka fabric. Looking into the king's eyes, she could see her radiant beauty held him spellbound. Swinging her arms twice wafted an ever so slight air of perfume over the king. Ahasuerus leaned forward in an effort to inhale the intoxicating scent. Suddenly, she dropped to her knees and bowed her head in respect. None of the other girls had thought to humble themselves before the king. Ahasuerus, like every prince of the realm, was speechless. Before anyone could utter a word, the seven attendants danced out, surrounded Esther, and skirted her away. Several moments later, excited chatter began.

Her plan had its desired effect. Anticipation had created male arousal. Fully revealing her body to the king alone, kneeling and bowing in submission, seized the prize. Esther was given the wardrobe of the former queen Vashti and brought into the court. Memucan escorted her to the queen's seat below the king's and handed Ahasuerus the crown. The king placed the crown on Esther's head and proclaimed her Queen of Persia.

During Esther's time in the care of Hegai, she dared not attempt any contact with Mordecai. Nonetheless, Mordecai sat at the palace gate day after day, hoping to receive word of her progress. Unbeknown to the king, or anyone else for that matter, a few influential people in the realm were not happy with the king's acceptance of the Jews and their appointment to many administrative positions. Mordecai had become such a fixture outside the palace gates; he was rarely noticed. One afternoon, he fell asleep, and when he woke, it was dark. Mordecai heard voices plotting against Ahasuerus. Glancing briefly around the gate, Mordecai was able to identify two of the men in the torchlight. To his surprise, they were the king's trusted eunuchs. Bigthana and Teresh. Try as he may, he could not see the face of the third man. However, Mordecai did take a mental note of his tall, slender body.

Now that Esther was queen, Mordecai could safely message her. He asked her to arrange an audience with the king. Bigthana and Teresh tried earnestly to discourage the audience as Mordecai was a Jew and not Persian. Esther bowed before Ahasuerus and told him how Mordecai had taken her in and raised her as his own after her parents had died.

She said, "My king, I will vouch for the integrity of this man who has patiently waited for many full moons for an audience with you."

Amid protest from the two eunuchs, the king said, "Bring Mordecai forward."

Mordecai related his story of how he had spent many days waiting to hear of the fate of Esther. He told of his overhearing a conspiracy to kill the king between three men and then pointed to Bigthana and Teresh as they tried to leave. Forcibly subdued, the eunuchs knew their fate was sealed. They broke loose and charged the king. It was a smart move. By doing so, they avoided enduring a horrible torture to reveal the third conspirator. In an instant, the schemers were cut down. After removing the bodies, Ahasuerus asked if Mordecai could identify the third conspirator. Not able to see the face of the third man, he told the king he could not.

The king looked around his court and then called, "Haman, where are you? Come forward."

Haman approached and bowed.

Ahasuerus proclaimed, "Haman, I commission you to find the third conspirator and name you Viceroy of the Persian Empire for that purpose."

When Haman stood, Mordecai began to shiver. The form of a tall, slender man standing with his back to him was very familiar. It was him, but unable to see the face that night, it meant certain death to falsely accused the newly appointed viceroy. Little did anyone know Haman hated the Jews with a passion.

Ahasuerus announced, "Let all those in my kingdom bow to Haman, my viceroy."

This troubled Mordecai. He knew he would not be able to bring himself to bow to the man he suspected of treason. Haman knew it would be dangerous to let Mordecai live even if he had not seen his face. Each time he saw Haman coming, Mordecai turned his back so that he would not have to bow. When others noticed how Mordecai refused to reverence Haman, they told him, and his wrath burned so that he wanted to slaughter every Jew in the kingdom. In the palace, Esther continued to please the king in every way possible. Ahasuerus was happy to have a beautiful and, more importantly, an obedient wife.

Haman approached the king and reported that he had found that all through the empire, there were people who despised the king's laws and were the ones behind the plot to kill him. He told the king these people should be destroyed and yet did not tell him that Mordecai was one of those people. A superstitious man, Haman enlisted the help of three elderly women to cast lots in order to determine the best day to carry out his plan. The day determined by the casting of lots, Haman pledged to give ten thousand talents of silver into the king's treasury. However, there was a condition that he be allowed to keep the property of those convicted of breaking the king's laws. It was agreed, and Ahasuerus set the day of the mass destruction for the thirteenth day of Adar, the first month. It was three full moons hence. Messengers took the king's decree to every governor in the empire. When the Jews learned of the plot, there was great wailing and gnashing of teeth in the land.

Esther heard that Mordecai had dressed in sackcloth and sat fasting and weeping over the decree at the king's gate. Her chamberlain Hatach was sent with clean clothing, but Mordecai refused. Hatach asked why. He was told how Haman deceived the king and was given power over life and death in the kingdom. Hatach was also given a copy of the decree and said he suspected Haman was the one behind the king's assassination attempt. The following day, Esther sent word back to Mordecai to gather all the Jews in the city in fasting and prayer. She would do the same with her servants and maidens. Mordecai had been waiting days to be permitted to bring his petition before the king. Years earlier, Ahasuerus had decreed that anyone coming before him without permission would be put to death. Day after day, Mordecai waited, but Haman made sure permission was never granted.

Esther sent a request, but Haman blocked it. Three days later, Esther put on her royal apparel and stood humbly in the court anti room with others who had been granted an audience. When Ahasuerus saw his queen, he waved the golden sceptre and bid her enter. Esther apologized and explained how she had organized a special luncheon for the king and his viceroy Haman three days hence, and begged him to attend. Feeling his authority had not been impinged upon, the king sent word to Haman, commanding him to come to the palace. Ahasuerus wanted to know how the plans for destroying the disobedient in the kingdom were coming and to extend Esther's invitation to him personally.

On entering the palace, Haman passed Mordecai, who sat in his way. When Mordecai did not stand or move, Haman felt an even greater indignation and contempt for this Jew. That evening, Haman related the indignity to his family and how he had to attend a banquet with Esther and the king in three days. His wife Zeresh suggested having gallows built and hanging Mordecai as a lawbreaker the day after the banquet. Haman sent for his servant and instructed him to have gallows built.

The strangest thing happened that night. Ahasuerus, who never had problems falling to sleep, could not. Try as he may, he finally called for Memucan, thinking, "I will have him read the chronicles of my recent deeds. Surely, they will put me to sleep."

As it came to pass, Memucan read the account of Mordecai identifying Bigthana and Teresh, the two eunuchs who had conspired to kill him.

The king asked, "What honor has been bestowed upon him for his service?"

"None," replied Memucan.

"I shall remedy that on the morrow."

Feeling a comforting peace fall over him, Ahasuerus fell off to sleep while Memucan continued reading.

The following day, Haman was summoned to the king's presence.

The king asked, "What shall be done unto the man whom the king delights to honor?"

Haman, thinking there could not possibly be anyone other than himself the king would want to honor, answered, "Cloth him in royal apparel. Seat him upon the king's horse, parade him through the streets and proclaim the honor due the man."

Ahasuerus stood and said, "Good, so let it be done. Take my royal apparel to Mordecai, who sits in sackcloth at the king's gate. Mount him upon my horse and let the proclamation begin."

That parade was the most horrible day of Haman's life. When he thought that it could not get any worse, one of Esther's servants arrived early the next morning to remind Haman of the noon banquet. Haman knew it was not wise to beg off with the king in attendance. Conversation was light, with Haman speaking only when asked an opinion. With the previous day a horrible experience, this day was about to turn into a nightmare.

Ahasuerus asked Esther, "What is thy petition, my queen."

"We are sold. My people and I are to be destroyed, and I plea for their pardon."

"Who is he, and where is he, that durst presume such a deed?"

Esther answered, "The enemy of my people."

"What enemy? I know of no enemy."

Enraged, Haman rose to indict Mordecai as disobedient to the king's laws. At that moment, Harbonah, one of the chamberlains, entered with news that Mordecai had come seeking an audience with his majesty. Haman stood frozen.

As Mordecai approached the king, Esther pointed and said, "Our enemy is the wicked is Haman."

"Nonsense!" shouted Haman as he hurried to the door.

Ahasuerus was confused but was able to shout, "Stop, you do not have permission to leave."

Mordecai knelt before the king and presented one of the decrees sent to the governors under the king's signet. It did not say that those who violated the king's laws were to be put to death and their property confiscated.

It read, "Put all Jews, women, and children, to death. Let their property be confiscated and deposited into my treasury."

While the king burnt with anger, Harbonah informed him of Haman's gallows, built to hang the Jew Mordecai.

Ahasuerus commanded, "Take the signet ring from him and give it to Mordecai."

Guards ripped the ring from Haman's finger.

The king continued, "Take the treasonous Haman and hang him on the gallows he had built for my loyal subject Mordecai."

To ensure future retribution unto Mordecai, Ahasuerus had Haman's ten sons and wife hanged that same day on the gallows Zeresh had Haman build.

Mordecai reminded the king of the decree and was commanded to prepare another in the king's name, rescinding the false proclamation. On the fourteenth day of Adar, Jews in the one hundred and twenty-seven provinces of the Persian Empire held a joyous festival celebrating the defeat of those who wished to destroy them. The festival was called Purim and named after Pur, the casting of lots. It represents the irony of the one who would destroy the Jews finding that he was the one to be destroyed. Haman had cast his lot against God's chosen people and lost. Purim is also when festivities are shared with the poor and unfortunate. For over twenty-five hundred years, Jews from around the world, the remnant of Israel, have celebrated this joyous festival.

The many stories from the shephelah range from the miraculous to the bizarre. Through it all, God has remained faithful to creation, enduring and forgiving all of their backslidings. Why? The only possible answer is God's love. You have heard my stories, and now I can rest easy knowing my account has reached the ears of the faithful.

Shalom my friend, Shalom.

THE END